Thomas Williams, Thomas Belsham

A Vindication of the Calvinistic Doctrine of Human Depravity

the atonement, divine influences, &c. - in a series of letters to the Rev. T. Belsham

Thomas Williams, Thomas Belsham

A Vindication of the Calvinistic Doctrine of Human Depravity
the atonement, divine influences, &c. - in a series of letters to the Rev. T. Belsham

ISBN/EAN: 9783337368708

Printed in Europe, USA, Canada, Australia, Japan

Cover: Foto ©Andreas Hilbeck / pixelio.de

More available books at **www.hansebooks.com**

A

VINDICATION

OF THE

CALVINISTIC DOCTRINES

OF

HUMAN DEPRAVITY, THE ATONEMENT,
DIVINE INFLUENCES, &c.

IN A SERIES OF

LETTERS

TO

The Rev. T. BELSHAM:

OCCASIONED BY

HIS "REVIEW OF Mr. WILBERFORCE's TREATISE."

WITH

AN APPENDIX

ADDRESSED TO

The AUTHOR of "LETTERS ON HEREDITARY DEPRAVITY."

―――――

By *THOMAS WILLIAMS*,
AUTHOR OF THE AGE OF INFIDELITY, &c.

―――――

The man whole iole fpring of action is a concern for luft fouls, and a care to preferve the
purity of that gofpel which alone teaches the moft effectual method of their recovery
from the power of fin and Satan unto God, will feel an ardour of mind that will prompt
him ftrenuoufly to op,ofe all thofe whom he confiders as obftructing his benevolent
defigns,—I could overlook every thing in a man who, I thought, mea^^nothing but my
everlafting welfare.   Mr. PALEY.

―――――

LONDON:

Printed for the AUTHOR by A. PARIS, Roll's Buildings;
And fold at No. 10, Stationers' Court, Ludgate Hill;
Sold alfo by Meffrs. CHAPMAN, Fleet-ftreet; MATTHEWS, Strand;
OGLE, Turnftile; HEPTINSTALL, Holborn; BUTTON, HURST,
and PARSONS, Paternofter-row; DICKIE, Bow-lane; and KNOTT,
Lombard-ftreet: JAMES, Briftol; and OGLE, Edinburgh and
Glafgow.

―――――

1799.
Price 4s. in Boards. Entered at Stationers Hall.

SIR,

BEFORE I began these Letters, I thought it necessary to enquire whether you had any similar design. Though your assurance to the contrary determined me to proceed, a variety of more pressing engagements retarded the publication. Should it in any degree subserve the cause of Evangelical Religion, those fragments of time which have been redeemed (or perhaps stolen) for the purpose, will not prove misemployed.

Averse as I am to party language, I have not been able wholly to avoid it. The term *Calviniſtic*, in particular, has, by various arts, been rendered odious; yet, under this term Unitarian Writers generally comprehend the doctrines of Human

man Depravity, the Atonement of Christ, and the Influences of the Holy Spirit, a circumstance which has obliged me to adopt it ; though I am sensible that these truths are no less dear to thousands who do not pass under the denomination of Calvinists.

As the following Defence originated in an attack on your ' Practical View,' you will, I flatter myself, excuse this liberty, and permit me, in addressing the Advocate of Religion and Humanity, the honour and privilege of subscribing myself

Your much obliged,

and moſt obedient ſervant,

Auguſt 1, 1799.　　　　THOMAS WILLIAMS.

CONTENTS.

APPENDIX,

Addreffed to the Author of ' Letters on Hereditary Depravity.

A

VINDICATION

OF THE

CALVINISTIC DOCTRINES.

LETTER I.

INTRODUCTORY.

Rev. Sir,

ALTHOUGH the avowal and vindication of his religious fentiments
is every man's birth-right, yet to appear
as the advocate of Mr. Wilberforce, or the
opponent of Mr. Belfham, may feem to require fome apology. The former character I have not the prefumption to affume:
it is only accidentally that I have noticed
that Gentleman's work, as having occa-
fioned your attack on principles equally dear
and important to me as to Mr. W. And
with refpect to the latter, if there be any

B   temerity

temerity in the attempt, it muſt ariſe from my. inferiority in the conteſt, which I ſhall be quite as willing to admit as you can be to aſſert ; and if the difference ſhould prove ten-fold in your favour, let it be remembered your advantage is proportionate, and no leſs ſo my claim on the candour of the Public.

It is equally favourable to your cauſe that your ſentiments are ſo flattering to human nature, and ſo palateable to the taſte of this *ſoi-diſant* Age of Reaſon : and this advantage is the greater if, as you inform us, there are many thouſands, both in the church and out of it, who are, at leaſt ſecretly, on your ſide *. A circumſtance I am the more ready to believe from what I know of the ſpread of infidelity.

In addreſſing your Letters to a *Lady*, you ſeem deſirous to ſtrengthen your intereſt farther by the patronage of the fair ſex, whoſe influence over us commences with the cradle and the breaſt, and continues commenſurate with the current of our lives. I confeſs that from my opinion of the piety

* Review, p. 227.

and

and intelligence of women (who have been often remarked to have more religion in general, than men), I fhould have no fear as to the refult of an appeal to their judgment; but I am perfuaded they have too much modefty to give an award on queftions of Theology.

Should it be enquired with what difpofition I enter upon this inveftigation; whether I feel that indifference to fentiment, which fome writers confider as a neceffary pre-requifite to a difcovery of truth—an indifference which makes it perfectly the fame to me whether my principles on examination prove true or falfe—I muft confefs that I am not thus indifferent: I have found that comfort and fatisfaction in them, that ' my heart's defire and prayer to God is,' that you, and my readers alfo, may enjoy the fame.—If this fhould appear unpromifing, permit me to afk, What would be thought of an advocate for Natural Religion, who fhould fet out with confeffing it a matter of perfect indifference to him, whether or not there were a God, or a divine providence ?—But you, Sir, need not be told that a regard to principles may con-

fift

lift with a juft fenfe of our own fallibility, and an opennefs to conviction by the arguments of an opponent. Whatever others may have advanced, you have, much to your honour, contended for the *importance* of *religious truth*. On this point, therefore, I may fuppofe we are agreed; I wifh we were equally fo as to what is truth.

Before I conclude this letter, permit me to mention one thing which has embarraffed me a little. I hate the illiberality of party names; and yet, in fpeaking of parties, I am obliged to ufe them. On my own fide I can find no difficulty, you and your friends have furnifhed me with a variety: we are Trinitarians, Calvinifts, Enthufiafts, and Chriftian Idolators *. All, or any of thefe names may do for us; but by what term fhall I diftinguifh the friends of your hypothefis?

The name *Socinian* you difavow; and Socinus would have difavowed you as an heretic, or an infidel; and probably have immured you in a prifon †. As to the

---

* Review, p. 129, 130.
† Toulmin's Life of Socinus, p. 105.

name

name *Unitarian*, I am unwilling exclusively
to allow it; because we believe in no more
gods than you do; yet, for diftinction's fake,
I muft be content to adopt this as a *popular* term for your *non-deſcript* denomination.

It is neceffary, however, to obferve, that
as by ufing thefe terms I do not wifh to
make you anfwerable for the fentiments of
other Unitarian Writers, fo neither do I
make myfelf refponfible for the opinions of
other Calvinifts, any farther than I have
avowed them. In general, my ideas corref-
pond with thofe of the great Reformer of
Geneva; but in all parties the fhades of difference in opinion are as numerous almoft
as the individuals who compofe them.

Having fettled thefe preliminaries, I fhall,
for the prefent, fubfcribe myfelf, in the
caufe of God and truth,

Your humble fervant,

T. W.

LETTER II.

On the Test of Truth.

Rev. Sir,

BEFORE we enter on the investigation of any particular point of faith, it is necessary that we agree upon certain *criteria* as our rule; otherwise we may wrangle without end, but shall make no progress in the search after truth. The only *criteria* I would employ in these Letters are *Reason* and the *Scriptures*.

I suppose we are agreed, that it is the province of *Reason* to judge of the evidences of Revelation, and of its import. I pretend not, any more than yourself, to be an inspired expositor: but being satisfied, after a due examination, that the scriptures commonly received by Protestants are genuine, I use my understanding to investigate their meaning, not without prayer that my faculties may be strengthened in the research, and my judgment chastened by divine in-

struction

struction. Perhaps you will accompany me in this, if no farther.

Having received full satisfaction on the divine authority of the Bible, I consider myself bound to submit, whenever it appears determinate and clear; without torturing the sacred writers by forced criticism, or conjectural emendation; and without presuming to cull only such precepts or doctrines as are agreeable to my inclination, or within the sphere of my comprehension. To instance in a single point: when I read of the Resurrection of the Dead, I think myself bound to receive it on the authority of the Revealer, altho' utterly incomprehensible, and implying innumerable circumstances totally dissimilar to any thing which I have witnessed; and, in my view, one of the greatest mysteries either in nature or christianity.

I fear we differ widely in our estimation of the *authority* of the sacred writers; but in order to meet you on your own principles, and for the sake of argument, I shall, in these Letters, insist only upon that degree of *authority* which you seem willing to allow them, ' as capable and faithful witnesses,

' both

' both of the doctrine which Jesus taught,
' and of the facts which they relate*.'

- To a critical investigation of the authen-
ticity and tranflation of particular paffages I
have no objection ; and am willing (fo far
as I may be able) to employ all the care
you recommend, to difcover their ' genuine
' fenfe, without taking into confideration
' whether it agrees with this, or is repugnant
' to that hypothefis of vain and ignorant men,
' who ftrain the apoftolic language to the
' fupport of their favourite fyftems.+.'

But though you acknowledge the Scriptures, critically examined, and rightly underftood, to be the teft of Truth, and complain of rational chriftians being ' often ac-
' cufed of not paying due refpect' to their
' authority ‡ ;' yet I obferve, that your manner of criticifing is fuch as to leave very little
in them, to which a mutual appeal can be
made.

On this principle you might well ob-
ferve, || that ' It would be difficult to prove
' that David in his penitential lamentation

' over his enormous crime, wrote under a
' divine impulfe, or that Solomon was fuper-
' naturally endowed with any other than
' political wifdom.' You might have added
on this principle, that it would be difficult to
prove that one hundreth part of the Bible is
infpired. On this ground, one need not be
furprifed at your making no ufe of it in judging of the divine character, but in the true
fpirit of infidelity, declaring, that ' we have
' no fatisfactory rule of judging of the cha-
' racter of the Deity, but from his operati-
' ons*;' in which it is manifeft, by what follows, you do not mean to include the Scriptures. Farther, you ' allow the infpiration of
' the writers ·of the New Teftament in no
' cafes where they do not themfelves *exprefs-
' ly claim* it +.' This appears to me very
unreafonable. An ambaffador having produced his credentials, expects to be accredi-
ted till he is recalled or fuperceded: A
fteward empowered to receive rents, produces his authority on the firft demand, but
does not expect it to be required every time:
A fervant empowered to open credits, and

receive payments, retains his power while he retains his fervice, unlefs his authority be withdrawn. So the apoftles were ambaffadors, ftewards, fervants of Jefus Chrift, and had a right to be refpected in their public character, wherever no intimations are given to the contrary, of which we have fome remarkable inftances in the Epiftles of Paul *; and thefe exceptions forcibly confirm the opinion of his writing in general under the influence of infpiration. However, in order to accommodate myfelf to the weaknefs of your faith, care fhall be taken as to the authority, as well as perfpicuity, of the evidence adduced by

Yours, &c.

* 1 Cor. vii. 6, 10, 12, 25, 26, 40.—xi. 17, &c.

LETTER III.

The Scripture Doctrine of the Depravity of Human Nature.

REV. SIR,

OUR firſt queſtion relates to a matter of fact. *Is human nature depraved, or not?* A queſtion I ſhould ſuppoſe unneceſſary with the friends of Revelation, ſince the evidence of the fact is ſo full and complete, that it pours around like day-light.

It abounds every where in the ſacred writings. MOSES not only gives the hiſtory of its origin in the fall, but delivers this ſentance, as from God himſelf, prior to the flood. ' And God ſaw that the wickedneſs ' of man was great in the earth, and that every ' imagination of the thoughts of his heart was ' only evil continually.' And it repented the ' Lord that he had made man on the earth, and ' it grieved him at his heart *.' As you, Sir, profeſs yourſelf a lover of criticiſm, permit me to remark, that there is an emphaſis, not

---

* Gen. vi. 5, 6.

only

only in the words themfelves, but in their grammatic form; in the original, the future tenfe being here ufed for the preter, or rather the *prefent* tenfe (which is deficient in the Hebrew), as often is the cafe where the fenfe is not reftrained to a particular period; and, if I am not greatly miftaken, this form of fpeaking denotes the character given to belong to every generation of mankind. For the truth of the propofition however, whether the criticifm be admitted or not, we have divine authority; for we find the Lord again declaring, immediately after the flood, that the human heart is ftill the fame: ' I will not again curfe the ' ground any more for man's fake; for the ' imagination of man's heart is evil from ' his youth *,'

DAVID

---

* Gen. viii. 21.—Some critics have been nibbling at this text by rendering the particle כי *although*, inftead of *for*; but admitting it fometimes to bear that rendering, there feems no occafion for here departing from its firft and primary fignification. " I will not add to curfe the earth any more (בעבור) on account of man; (כי) becaufe the thoughts of the heart of man are evil from his youth." Here the two Hebrew particles are evidently fynonimous; God would not curfe the earth any
more

DAVID and SOLOMON may be writers of little weight with you. Poſſibly you will admit, however, that they had ſome knowledge of human nature, and of their own hearts. The former confeſſes himſelf to be ' ſhapen in iniquity and conceived in ' ſin * ;' and the latter witneſſes, that ' God ' made

more *on account* of man—*becauſe* of the wickedneſs of his heart, &c.

The argument, however, does not reſt upon a criti-ciſm. Admitting the propoſed rendering of *although*, ſtill it ſuppoſes the fact, that ' the thoughts of the heart of man *are* evil from his youth.'

* Pſ. li. 5. Rather, more literally and accurately,
' Behold, in iniquity was I BORN;
' Yea, in ſin did my mother CONCEIVE me.'

Mr. Bulkley, in his late Apology for Human Na-ture, ſeems to intimate as if this was ſome misfortune peculiar to David, conveying an oblique reflection on his mother; but afterwards, as if conſcious of this being unfounded, and aſhamed of the innuendo, he tries to explain it away in another manner; as if he had ſaid, ' Were ſuch a thing *any way poſſible*, I could even be-lieve myſelf to have been born with a *propenſity to ſin.*' Is not this ſaying that the Pſalmiſt had felt ſo ſtrong a propenſity to ſin that he knew not how other-ways to account for it ? And that, admitting the poſſibility of original ſin, it was certainly the beſt and only method to ſolve the problem ? But after all, we are told it is only a ſtrong

'·made man upright, but they have fought
' out many inventions'—' yea, alfo the heart
' of the fons of men is full of evil, and mad-
' nefs is in their heart *.'

The Prophets, in general, feem deeply
affected with this humbling truth; and
JEREMIAH, in particular, delivers the following oracle from the mouth of God himfelf: ' The heart is deceitful above all
' things, and defperately wicked; who can
' know it? I the Lord fearch the heart
' and try the reins,' &c. As if the Lord
had faid, ' None but myfelf, whofe prero-
' gative it is to fearch the heart, can com-
' prehend the depth of its iniquity †.'

JESUS CHRIST himfelf, whom you admit
to be ' a teacher fent from God,' expreffes
the fame doctrine, in terms at leaft equally
clear and ftrong: ' From within, out of the

---

a ftrong poetical or proverbial expreffion; as if one fhould,
fay, ' Surely I was mad—out of my fenfes, or bewitched!'
A very proper illuftration to fuch a comment, and very
much à propos! See Bulkley's Apol. p. 78.—81.

* Ecclef. vii. 29. ix. 3.

† Jer. xvii. 9, 10. ' Defperately wicked' הוא אנש
depravity itfelf.—אנש Enoſh, is a man depraved, fallen,
mortal.

' heart,'

' heart,' fays he, not pointing to any individual, but to the fpecies—' Out of the
' heart of men proceed evil thoughts, adul-
' teries, fornications, murders, thefts, co-
' vetuoufnefs, wickednefs, deceit, lafcivi-
' oufnefs, an evil eye, blafphemy, pride,
' foolifhnefs : all thefe evil things come
' from within, and defile the man *.'

Once more, PAUL, the difciple of Gama-
liel, but who afterward received his doctrine
from the Lord himfelf †, gives the following
account of the ftate of human nature ; part
of which being quoted from the Pfalms,
unites the authority of the Prophet with that
of the Apoftle. Speaking ' both of Jews and
Gentiles,' Paul fays, ' They are all under
' fin.'—' As it is written, " there is none
" righteous ; no, not one : There is none
" that underftandeth, there is none that
" feeketh after God. They are all gone
" out of the way ; they are altogether be-
" come unprofitable : there is none that
" doeth good, no, not one." Then, after
enumerating particulars, he fays, ' Now we
' know that what things foever the law

---

* Mark, vii. 21—23.   † Gal. i. 1, 12.

' faith,

' faith, it faith to them that are under the
' law : that EVERY MOUTH may be ftopped,
' and ALL THE WORLD become guilty be-
' fore God *.'

Now, Sir, will you permit me to place

* Rom. iii. 9---19. Though I have not inferted it
in the text, I am much inclined to admit the fug-
geftion of a friend, that by thofe who ' are under the
'law,' Paul intended the Ifraelites, in diftinction from
the world; and that he meant to reafon from the depravity of that chofen nation to that of the whole
world. Having in the firft chapter proved the Gentiles to be wicked in the extreme : the only exception
that could be pleaded was that of the Jews.----Are
they no better? He allows, chap. ii. that they had
greater advantages than the others, in being favoured
with a divine Revelation, &c. yet did they not practice what they knew, nor did the goodnefs of God
lead (or influence) them unto repentance, ver. 17---
23. Chap. iii. he then afks, where is the difference
between Jew and Gentile? They differ in advantages, but not in character. Hear their own fcriptures, ver. 9---18. Thefe things are not faid of ignorant heathens, but of God's own nation; for what the
law, or Jewifh fcripture faith, it faith to thofe that
are under the law, i. e. to the Jews : and if they are
thus depraved and wicked, where fhall we find the
good? Every mouth muft be ftopped, and all the
world become guilty before God.---This view of the
paffage ftrengthens my argument, but is not effential
to its validity.

under

under thefe quotations your own opinion?
That ' there is upon the whole a very great
' preponderence of good in general, and
' with few, if any exceptions, in every in-
' dividual in particular *.' And let me afk
what reafon will you give that your word,
and that of a few other modern philofophers,
is to be preferred to the folemn decifion of
prophets, apoftles, and Jefus Chrift himfelf?

I have faid *modern* philofophers, becaufe
the antients clearly are againft you. Dr.
Doddridge, who will be admitted to have
been well acquainted with their writings,
and certainly a man of candour, fays—
' Thofe who have carefully ftudied human
' nature, even amongft *pagans*, have acknow-
' ledged (and that in *very ftrong* terms) an
' inward depravation and corruption, adding
' a difproportionate force to evil examples,
' and rendering the mind averfe to good †.'

On the general queftion of the depravity
of human nature, Mr. Wilberforce has very

* Review. p. 13.

† Doddridge's Lectures, vol. ii. p. 198. Kippis's
edition. Alfo Hiftoric Defence, vol. i. chap. 6.

properly

properly appealed to facts, and ' facts are stubborn things.' He has ably and elo- quently argued from a variety of topics equally popular and convincing. I have no desire to repeat his arguments, and it seems the more unnecessary as you have replied to them only in a few instances, which I shall notice as we proceed.

I cannot omit this opportunity of observing the expedients to which you are frequently driven, in attempting to account for the language of Scripture on this subject. ' The Jews (you tell us) having been chosen ' by God to peculiar privileges, entertained ' a very high notion of their own dignity, ' and expressed themselves in the most con- ' temptuous language of the idolatrous Gen- ' tiles, who were not in covenant with ' Jehovah. Of themselves they spoke as a " *chosen* and a *holy nation, sons of God*, and " *heirs of the promises.*' But the heathens ' were represented as ' *sinners*, as *aliens*, as " *enemies* to *God*,' and the like. In allusion ' to which forms of expression, the con- ' verted Gentiles being entitled equally ' with converted Jews, to the blessings of ' the new dispensation, they are therefore

' said

' faid to be *forgiven, reconciled,* and *faved,*
' to be ' *fellow-citizens* with the faints, and
" of the houfehold of God *."

So then, Sir, the Gentiles only were finners and enemies to God ; and thefe not in
reality, but in the prejudiced opinion of the
felf righteous Jews ; and thefe prejudices
were carried fo far as to be mingled with
the chriftian doctrine of falvation ; and we
are *forgiven, reconciled,* and *faved,* only by a
Jewifh conceit ! A happy way this of explaining Scripture phrafes ; and, if I miftake
not, fome improvement on the method of
Dr. Taylor !

But to be ferious—as the fubject certainly
requires, though your gloffes fcarcely will
permit—Do the facred writers afcribe the
terms finners, enemies to God, &c. *only* to
the Gentiles ? Did not Jefus Chrift declare
that it fhould be more tolerable for Sodom
and Gomorrah than for unbelieving Jews ?—
Did not Paul renounce all moral pre-emin-
ence of the Jews above the Gentiles ? ' Are
' we better than they ?' faid he ; ' No, in
' no wife.'—Did not Peter charge upon the

---

* Review, p. 17, 18.

Jews

Jews the enormous fin of crucifying the
Lord of glory?—What then can you mean
by infinuating, that the apoftles in the ufe
of thefe terms wrote under the influence
of Jewifh prejudices; and when they called
the Gentiles *finners*, &c. did not mean to
include themfelves?

I rifk nothing in faying that the oppofite
to this is expreffed, in terms as clear and
unequivocal as any language can furnifh.
Paul, in particular, exprefsly fays, that between Jew and Gentile, in the bufinefs of
falvation, ' there is NO difference ; for ALL
' have *finned*, and come fhort of the glory of
' God *.' Alfo in writing to the Ephefians,
fo far from making an illiberal, diftinction
between his countrymen and thofe Gentile
converts, he exprefsly includes *himfelf*, who
was an Hebrew of the Hebrews, and a
Pharifee. ' You (faith he) hath he quicken-
' ed, who were dead in trefpaffes and fins,
' wherein, in times paft, ye walked, accord-
' ing to the courfe of this world, according
' to the prince of the power of the air, the
' fpirit that now worketh in the children of

---

* Rom. iii. 22, 23.

difcbe-

' difobedience : among whom WE ALL had
' OUR converfation in times paft, in the
' lufts of OUR flefh, fulfilling the defires of
' the flefh, and of the mind; and were BY
' NATURE the CHILDREN OF WRATH
' EVEN AS OTHERS.' Now, Sir, in whatever fenfe the terms *by nature* and *children
of wrath* are here ufed, it is certainly clear,
that they apply equally to Jews and Gentiles; and, if it were poffible to doubt this
in the words here cited, the fubfequent context would demonftrate it; for there ' the
' partition wall' between Jews and Gentiles
is broken down, and both are ' raifed to-
' gether' to the privileges of chriftianity.
But you, Sir, tell us this paffage means nothing more than that the perfons to whom
he wrote had been originally Gentiles, en-
flaved like others to the idolatries and vices
of their heathen ftate *. That is, ' WE
[Paul and his converted *Jewifh* brethren;
—' we] Jews, were formerly idolatrous
' Gentiles !' If this be a fpecimen of *rational* criticifm, and *we* muft fignify *you*, and *I*
a third perfon, whenever the caufe of

* Review, p. 44.

Unitarianifm

Unitarianiſm requires it, there is an end to all certainty of ſcripture interpretation. If indeed the penmen of the New Teſtament wrote thus vaguely, they deſerve all the contempt you caſt on them ; but if they wrote like men of common ſenſe and honeſty (waving the queſtion of their inſpiration), the opprobrium recoils on your ſyſtem ; and your art of criticiſm is the art of ſhewing how little the ſcriptures may be made to mean.

Finally, Sir, permit me to appeal to your own obſervation and experience. I will not aſk, whether you be wholly inſenſible of innate depravity ? This might appear impertinent : but did you ever meet with a wiſe and good man, who pretended to be ſo.—As far as my inquiries have extended, I have found men of the moſt liberal ſentiments, the moſt amiable tempers, the moſt benevolent hearts, and the moſt uſeful lives—I have uniformly found theſe always ready to acknowledge and lament the fact. *Doddridge,* I have already cited. *Watts* (juſtly repreſented by Dr. Knox, as one of the moſt perfect of human characters) mingles it with all his ſongs. The benevolent

volent *Hanway* fays, ' Thofe know but
' little of the human heart who do not per-
' ceive an evident inconfiftency in it. No
' one can be ignorant that there is a perpe-
' tual ftruggle between his good and evil
' propenfities. This feems to mark out, in
' the ftrongeft characters, our being fallen
' from fomething we originally were, agree-
' able to what is related in the facred writ-
' ings of the fall of man.'—He adds (farther on), ' Our hearts are treacherous, and
' we cannot eafily fathom the depth of our
' own corruption *.'

To name but one other, a man of fuch
excellency as to be univerfally efteemed an
ornament to human nature, *Howard* the
philanthropift; this man, when he found
the nation meant to honour him with a
premature monument, immediately and re-
folutely oppofed it †.—' Alas ! (faid he) our
' beft performances have fuch a mixture of
' fin and folly that praife is vanity, and
' prefumption, and pain, to a thinking

* Hanway's Reflections on Life and Religion, vol. ii.
p. 412, 458.

† Stennet's Funeral Sermon for Howard.

' mind.'

' mind.'—Such are the opinions of the *beſt* men on the ſtate of human nature !

I ſhould here certainly introduce the apoſtle Paul again, as confeſſing and bewailing his natural depravity and conſequent infirmities, ' O wretched man that I ' am !' &c. but I expeⅽt you would put him to critical torture, by making him ſpeak in a falſe and aſſumed charaⅽter; and I have been already ſo much diſguſted by this violence to common ſenſe and truth, that I chooſe rather to let him reſt in peace.

I hope I have ſaid enough to prove, if any regard be due to ſcripture or experience, that mankind are univerſally depraved; now permit me to aſk, if you knew any one family which, from generation to generation, and in every variety of climate and of country, were ſubjeⅽt to a particular diſorder, would not this be ſufficient to prove that diſorder *natural* and conſtitutional ? Surely then, if all mankind, in every age, country, and ſituation, and from their earlieſt youth are contaminated more or leſs with ſin, this is abundantly ſufficient

ent to prove the diſorder is originally ſeated in human nature *.

Under a proper impreſſion of my own ſhare in this depravity, and with a becoming ſenſe of my infirmity, I deſire to ſubſcribe myſelf

Yours, &c.

---

* Pref. *Edwards*, in his " Chriſtian Doctrine of Original Sin," (Part I. chap. i. ſect. 2.) has proved and illuſtrated this univerſal propenſity to ſin with great variety of argument. I ſhould have quoted him at length, had not the caſe appeared too obvious to require it : but I take the liberty of ſaying in this place, that whatever on this ſubject may be found too ſlightly treated in my brief ſketch, may be found argued at length in that work with a force of reaſon, that to me appears nothing ſhort of demonſtration.

E

LETTER IV.

Mr. Belsham's View of the present State of Human Nature.

REV. SIR,

THE doctrine of human depravity is confessedly so much a fundamental principle, that I entered farther into the proof of it than perhaps was necessary, when my object is not to write a series of theological essays, or a body of divinity; but only to obviate some objections, and remove the stumbling blocks which you have thrown in the way of truth; however, my last letter was too long to admit an apology, and this may be better employed than in attempting one.

That there is a defect in the human character, and a degree of moral evil in the world, you seem willing to allow, by endeavouring to account for it, in consistency with your hypothesis. Men are not absolutely free from evil, you admit; but then they are good characters upon the whole, though not perfect ones. ' Character (you observe) is

' the

' the fum total of habits; but in forming an
' eftimate of moral worth, it is an invariable
' principle that *one* vice ftamps a character
' vicious, while a thoufand virtues will not
' atone for one immoral habit. If a man be
' a liar, or difhoneft, or intemperate, or im-
' pious, his character is denominated vicious,
' with whatever virtues it may otherwife be
' adorned. He who keepeth the whole law,
' and offendeth " in one point, is guilty of
" all." And the reafon is evident, virtue is
' that fyftem of habits which conduces to
, the greateft ultimate happinefs; vice is
' that which diminifhes happinefs, or pro-
' duces mifery. The union, therefore, of a
' fingle vice with a conftellation of virtues,
' will contaminate them all; will prevent
' them from producing their proper effect,
' and will, in proportion as it prevails, di-
' minifh the happinefs, or produce the mi ·
' fery of the agent, who never can attain
' the true end of his exiftence till this vice
' is eradicated.

' Hence it follows, that there may be a
' confiderable preponderance of virtues, even
' in characters juftly eftimated as vicious;
' and likewife, that the *quantity* of virtue
' in

' in the world may far exceed that of vice,
' though the *number* of virtuous characters
' may be less than that of vicious ones *.'

A little farther on, you add, ' Few cha-
' racters are flagrantly wicked; and perhaps
' even in the *worst* of men, good habits
' and actions are more numerous than the
' contrary. Certainly they are so in the
' majority of mankind, and .... preponderant
' virtue is almost universal†.'

This you consider as ' the real state of
' things :' how far it differs from the statement of the sacred writers may be seen by
comparing it with my last letter ; how far it
is consistent with itself, and with common
sense, is the point now to be examined.

1. If ' one vice stamp a character vicious,'
and that ' justly,' it must be because it renders it so. There must be something in
the indulgence of this one vice that gives
an immoral tinge to the whole mass of dis-
position, or as you express it, ' which con-
taminates all.' This is doubtless the truth :
for he that indulges one sin proves that it is
not from any regard to God, but merely

---

* Review, p. 37, 38.   † Ibid, p. 39.

owing

owing to the influence of fome felfifh motive that he is deterred from others. A difobedient fon may not live in the practical violation of *all* his father's commands; but if he continually allow himfelf to violate one, that is a fufficient proof, it is not from regard to parental authority, but with a view to his credit or intereft, that he complies with the others; and confequently, there is no principle of obedience in him. It is thus that ' he who offendeth in one point' of the law is said to be ' guilty of all *.' One allowed tranfgreffion deftroys the authority of the lawgiver, and with that the principle of obedience: for ' he that faith do not commit adultery, faith alfo, do not kill; now if thou commit no adultery, yet if thou kill, thou art become a tranfgreffor of the law.' So we may reafon, If thou doft not indulge intemperate anger, yet if thou indulgeft pride †; or if thou fubdueft pride, if

---

* James ii. 10.

† I recollect but one inftance of any perfon claiming an exemption from this mafter vice (pride) and that was Dr. Brown, the author of *Religio Medici*, and it has been univerfally confidered as a proof of his exceffive vanity.

thou

thou doft not fubdue anger, thou art become a tranfgreffor of the law, and a violator of the authority of the legiflator.

In perfect confiftency with this, the fcriptures reprefent it as impoffible for thofe that are ' in the flefh,' or under the dominion of vicious propenfities, to pleafe God *, as it is for an evil tree to bring forth good fruit. Thofe that bring forth good fruit are good trees : fo ' he that doeth righteoufnefs is righteous.' Now if thefe things be true (and they appear to refult neceffarily from your own premifes), what becomes of that ' conftellation of virtues,' which you find even in vicious characters, and on which ,refts your whole argument for the preponderance of virtue in the world ?

In what you fay of vice, either in men or children, being ' a deviation from the ac- ' cuftomed order of things,' you make virtue to confift in the mere appearance of it, or in abftaining from grofs immoralities, irrefpective of the motive; whereas you cannot be ignorant, that it is from *this* moral actions are determined good or evil. Accord-

* Rom. viii. 8.

ing

ing to your reafoning a man may do righteoufnefs, yea many acts of righteoufnefs to
one of wickednefs, and yet not be righteous.
Your good fruit confeffedly fprings from a
bad tree, which evinces that, however bene-
ficial it may prove in fociety, it is not good in
his fight whofe judgment is ever according
to the truth.

Not only are you defective in your ideas
of virtue, but vague and unfcriptural in your
ideas of vice. Were every man good and
honeft who efcapes a prifon, or avoids the
penalty of the laws, there might, indeed, be
fome plaufibility in your eftimate of the preponderance of virtue. But if according to
the doctrine of Jefus, every man that looks
luftfully upon a woman committeth adultery,
and every one unjuftly, or inordinately angry
is a murderer; if (as will follow from the
fame principle) every man who forms the
the wifh to deceive his neighbour is a liar,
and he who aims to defraud him is difhoneft; where then fhall we find your boafted
preponderance of virtue, and your great majority of good and virtuous men? On the
contrary, I fear we muft borrow the lantern
of Diogenes, or rather the candle of the Prophet

phet *, to find here and there a good and pious character.

2. If character be the fum total of habits, or (which is the fame thing) if the majority of habits, upon the fum total being efti-mated, denominate character, then where the habits of virtue preponderate above thofe of vice, the character may be denominated virtuous; and if good habits and actions are more numerous than the contrary, as you fay ' they certainly are in the majority of ' mankind,' it follows that the majority of mankind are certainly virtuous characters; and not the majority only, but the *whole*; for you think ' there may be a confiderable prepon-' derence of virtue, even in characters juftly ' eftimated as vicious, and perhaps in the ' worft of men:' but how you reconcile thefe fuppofitions with each other, and efpecially with the affertions of Scripture, and in par-ticular, with that of JESUS CHRIST, that many walk in the broad road of vice, and few in the narrow way that leads to life †, I confefs myfelf utterly unable to conceive.

* Zeph. i. 12.   † Matt. vii. 13.

3. Admit

3. Admitting that part of your premifes, that ' one vice ftamps a character vicious,' I fhould rather infer, that inftead of a majority of *virtuous* habits and actions in the *worft* men, we fhould find a majority of *vicious* habits and actions, even in the *beft* men. And thus the facred writers uniformly reprefent the fact. ' In many things we ' all offend—he that offendeth in one point ' is guilty of the whole,' &c.

' Who,' faith DAVID, ' can underftand ' his errors? cleanfe thou me from fecret ' faults.—Mine iniquities have taken hold ' upon me, fo that I am not able to look ' up: they are more in number than the ' hairs of mine head, therefore my heart ' faileth me.' Under the deepeft contrition he was fo far from thinking of the preponderance of his virtues, that he ufes language fuiting only the lips of a polluted creature ; " Create in me a clean heart O God, and " renew a right fpirit within me *." The apoftle PAUL is one of the moft moral characters in the fcriptures, yet he not only confeffes himfelf a finner, but the very chief†

---

* Pf. xix. 12. xl. 12. li. 10. † 1 Tim. i. 15, 16.

F

of

of finners, and a diftinguifhed inftance of forgiving grace.

It is true, that the fcriptures fpeaks of faints as well as finners ; and while they reprefent *all* men as guilty and depraved, fpeak of *fome* as good men, righteous, holy ; but then, it is in confequence of a moral, or rather of a fpiritual, change wrought in them :—they are *made* good, juftified, and fanctified ; operations, Sir, to which you unhappily confefs yourfelf a ftranger, and muft therefore feek another way to explain the paradox.

4. It may not be amifs to examine the character of thefe excellent virtues, and your very *courtly* definition of virtue from its *utility*.—I know that fome perfons judge every action to be right which they find ufeful, or convenient; and thus make their own intereft the criterion of right and wrong. But, I think, we have a far better teft in the will of our Creator, regulated according to the eternal fitnefs of things ; though, at the fame time, I admit that fuch is the original conftitution of providence, that our duty is always in unifon with our beft interefts, and conduces to our final happinefs

pinefs. Neverthelefs, it is dangerous and
injudicious to eftablifh this as the criterion
of right and wrong, becaufe, in many cafes,
it is far more difficult to determine what
mode of conduct is conducive to our happinefs, or to the general benefit of mankind,
than to afcertain our duty, which is commonly plain and clear : this, therefore,
would be explaining what is eafy by what is
difficult and obfcure.

The definition of virtue as a ' fyftem of
' habits,' is alfo remarkably inaccurate for
a writer of your talents. There are virtuous principles, habits, and actions, but thefe
fhould not be confounded with each other.
In a *general* view, virtue may comprehend
the whole; in a proper and *diftinctive* fenfe
it refers, I conceive, rather to the *principle*
than to the habit, or the conduct.

You proceed—' Children, we are told, [by
Mr. Wilberforce] "are perverfe and forward;"
' that is, they now and then difcover fuch
' a temper *.' If you are a father, Sir, which
I know not, and this is the extent of your
obfervation, I may pronounce you a happy
father, and your children happy-tempered

* Review, p. 39.

children

children. But a writer of more experience, and (if I may fpeak it without offence) of fuperior wifdom, has informed us, that " Foolifhnefs is bound (up) in the heart of " a child *." And truly, there is a per-verfenefs in the tempers of moft children, not eafily to be accounted for on any other principle than that of human depravity. But as this is rather a fubject of experience than of reafoning, I fhall content myfelf with appealing to the hearts of parents.

' Honefty,' you fay, ' affumes the name ' of *common* honefty from its general pre-' valence:' and this is the reafon, I fuppofe, that it is fo little valued; for, to fay a man poffeffes *common* honefty, is tantamount to faying he is half a rogue. So *mere* morality is cheap enough, for, as that term is commonly underftood, it implies the ab-fence of all true religion.

As to the doctrine, that ' all actions and ' habits, previous to converfion, are finful ;' it proceeds on principles fo juft and obvious, that I think you very happy in the expedi-ent you have adopted to get rid of it, by the affuring us that the refutation of ' fuch an

* Prov. xxii. 15.

' abfurdity

‘ abſurdity would be an abuſe of argument.’
Here, indeed, you are right enough, for it
is only by the ‘ abuſe of argument’ that
it could be refuted. The whole abſurdity,
however, lies in believing that man, with a
heart at enmity with God, can do nothing
in that ſtate with a view to pleaſe him, and
conſequently, nothing that is well pleaſing
to him :—or in the emphatic language of
Jeſus Chriſt, that ‘ an evil tree cannot
‘ bring forth good fruit.’ A doctrine that
you will not find it ſo eaſy to prove an abſurdity as to call it one.

That the narratives of the creation and
fall are literally true, I have no doubt ; but
it is not neceſſary to my preſent deſign to
inveſtigate them, and the attempt would
greatly extend my plan. That we ſome
way or other become partakers of the guilt
of our firſt parents, and ſubject to its conſequences, is, what I ſhould have ſuppoſed
no chriſtian miniſter would deny ; but it is
become faſhionable to advance bold and dar-
ing paradoxes ; and nothing has a greater
effect with many readers. I will leave it,
however, to your judgment to determine,
whether it be moſt reaſonable to believe that

we

we partake of pain and ficknefs, and death, which are the wages of fin, from Adam, on account of our being related to him, and fome way implicated in his crime ; or whether we partake the penalty without any participation of the fault.—Leaving this to your confideration and enquiries, I again fubfcribe myfelf

Yours, &c.

LETTER V.

The Origin of Human Depravity.

REV. SIR,

YOU have raifed two grand objections to the doctrine of Human Depravity, as ftated by Calvinifts:

1, That if moral evil be natural and neceffary it muft be the work of God, in fuch
a manner as to make him anfwerable for it.

2. That if a *majority* of evil prevail, it
imputes malevolence to the Creator.—Both
thefe inferences appear to me blafphemous;
either then the premifes, or the conclufion,
muft, in my view, be erroneous.

The formal difcuffion of thefe propofi-
tions would naturally involve the grand
queftion of the origin of evil; an enquiry
upon which I dare not enter. It was indeed too great for Milton, and for Milton's
angels, at leaft when fallen; who

———————————"Reafon'd high
" Of Providence, foreknowledge, will and fate;
" Fix'd fate, free-will, foreknowledge abfolute;
" And found no end, in wand'ring mazes loft *."

* Paradife Loft, book ii. line 558.

All

All I fhall attempt in *this* letter, is merely to offer a few obfervations on your firft
objection, and the reafonings by which you
fupport it.

Firft, In the axiom which you have affumed from the words of a fuppofed objector, that ' whatever we are *by nature*, we
' are what our Creator made us *,' you
have availed yourfelf of the *ambiguity* of a
term to mifreprefent the fentiments of your
opponents.   The term *nature*, as applied to
man, properly fignifies that which belongs
to his frame or conftitution *as man :* but, it
is alfo ufed for a mere accidental property,
in cafes where that property comes into the
world, and grows up with us, in oppofition
to properties contracted by imitation or
cuftom.   Thus, fome perfons feem at leaft, by
your own acknowledgement +, ' to inhe-
' rit the vices, as well as the difeafes of their
' parents ;' and where this is the cafe, it is
common to fay, they are *ill-natured*, or that
evil is ingrained (as it were) in their very
nature.   You well know, Sir, that it is not
in the firft fenfe, but in the laft, that we

* Rev. p. 81.   † Ib. p. 11.

confider

confider men as depraved *by nature*. We do not believe that fin is an effential property of human nature ; but merely an accidental one : not produced by the Creator, but contracted by the creature *.

You are certainly aware that Calvinifts do not confider the ftate in which men are now born into the world, as being the fame with that in which they were originally created. They believe, from what they confider as the higheft authority, that " God made man " upright, after his own image—in the " likenefs of God made he him ;" but that by means of the fin of our firft parent, the whole fpecies is become polluted. This connexion they allow to have been eftablifhed by a divine conftitution : even by that fundamental law of nature, that *like produces like*. By this law the branch refembles the ftem, the ftream the fountain, and a

---

* I have fometimes thought, that much of the difficulty on this fubject arifes from fpeaking of fin as a pofitive being ; whereas, it is only a negative affection of being, and is accordingly generally expreffed in the New Teftament by terms of a negative import, as (Ανομια) illegality, or tranfgreffion ;—(Αμαρτια) miffing our aim, &c.

G   de-

degenerate, mortal, finful parent produces
a degenerated, mortal, finful offspring.
' Who,' faith Job, ' can bring a clean
' thing out of an unclean ?—What is man
' (faith Eliphaz) that he fhould be clean ?
' or he that is born of a woman, that he
' fhould be righteous * ?'

In this difpenfation of providence, we do
not, however, confider the Deity as anfwerable for the defects, infirmities, or faults of
his creatures. You, Sir, may object to this
view of things, and may charge it with abfurdity, and us with the want of underftanding; but you have no right to impute
your conclufions to us, as axioms, or allowed principles.

---

* Job xiv. 4. xv. 14. I have quoted thefe only
as aphorifms of the ancients; but I fee your endeavour (p. 48) to fet afide the teftimony of Eliphaz, by
obferving, that Jehovah cenfured him as having ' not
' fpoken the thing that was right.' You can hardly,
however, fuppofe this the point in queftion, becaufe
here we fee Job and his friend were perfectly agreed.
Befides, the point alluded to was evidently the providence of God, and not the condition of mankind.
' You have not fpoken of ME,' faith the Lord, ' the
thing that is right.' If Job's friends believed this
doctrine, however, it is, at leaft, a proof of its antiquity.

Secondly,

Secondly, The arguments which you have advanced againſt our principles are equally directed againſt your own. You ſay, 'It is futile to alledge, as a palliation of the 'difficulty, that the firſt parents of the hu-'man race were originally innocent and 'happy; but that, in conſequence of their 'fall, they contracted a depraved nature, 'which they tranſmitted to their poſterity, 'for which God is not acccuntable. Such 'reaſoning as this cannot impoſe upon the 'underſtanding even of a child. Did God 'reſign the direction of his works as ſoon as 'he had placed Adam in paradiſe? Is not 'his agency as really, and as immediately 'concerned in the formation of every indi-'vidual, as in that of their original anceſ-'tors? If I am born into the world a de-'praved creature, it is by his appointment, 'and even by his immediate energy, ' I am "what my Creator made me *."

That divine providence extends to the perſons and poſterity of Adam, and that divine energy is continually exerted in carrying into effect the eſtabliſhed laws of nature, is

* Review, p. 32, 33.

readily

readily allowed : but does it follow from
hence, that God is ' accountable' for the
creatures' fin ? If fo, it will follow equally
from your own principles as from ours.
Whether men become finners in confequence
of the fall or not, finners they are, without
exception : and if we fuppofe with you, that
they are ' the creatures of circumftances,
' and that the habits they form are the refult
' of the impreffions to which they are ex-
' pofed *;' ftill the divine providence having
placed them in thofe circumftances, God
would be equally anfwerable for the creatures' fin, whether it arife from their orgin-
al, or fubfequent fituation. Indeed you feem
to have no objection to this confequence,
when you fay, ' The only enquiry of im-
' portance upon this fubject, is into the *quan-*
' *tity* and proportion of the evil which ac-
' tually exifts. How it was firft introduced
' is a queftion comparatively of little mo-
' ment. The difficulty is *the fame upon all*
' *hypothefes.* All muft ultimately be referred
' to God †.'

Thirdly, The moft important difference

----

* Review, p. 41.   † Ibid.

between us, relative to thefe fubjects, refpects the Creator being confidered as ' ac-
' countable for the fins of the creature.'
Whatever certain neceffarian Philofophers *
may have advanced, it is well known that
Calvinifts agree in rejecting this idea as blafphemous. We afcribe the government of
human volitions, as well as actions, to the
Supreme Being: but do not confider any influence to which we are expofed, as deftroy-
ing our free agency, and accountablenefs.
Judas in betraying Chrift, and the Jews in
putting him to death, did no more than
God's ' hand and counfel determined be-
' fore to be done :' yet, neverthelefs, ' by
' wicked hands he was crucified and
' flain †.' The Son of man went, as was
determined ; yet a heavy woe was denounced on him by whom he was betrayed.

But, Sir, your manner of reafoning appears
to afcribe the fins of men to the Creator in
fuch a fenfe as to render *him* ' accountable,'
rather than the creature. If divine providence extends over all events, you infer that
it is abfurd to reprefent Adam as contracting

* See Prieftley's Doctrine of Philofophical Neceffity. Sect. x.   † Acts ii. 23. iv. 28.

any

any fin, or tranfmitting it to his pofterity, 'for which God is not accountable.' So decidedly are you in favour of the finner, that, on the fuppofition of his inheriting a corrupt nature from Adam, (which, after all, you elfewhere treat as a matter of little moment) you fcruple not openly to efpoufe his caufe. You fide with the bold objector introduced by Mr. Wilberforce, juftify him throughout, and as if his expreffions were not ftrong enough, you encreafe their energy. Why, Sir, did you not alfo efpoufe the caufe of Paul's objector, and fay with him, ' Why ' doth he yet find fault; who hath refifteth ' his will?' You muft furely perceive the great refemblance between his language and the axiom to which you are fo partial—" I " am what my Creator made me."

Why did you not become the advocate of Judas, and of the murderers of Jefus Chrift? They were, as you fuppofe, ' the creatures ' of circumftances,' and their characters formed by the influences to which they were expofed, all which muft ' ultimately be re- ' ferred to God.' You could, doubtlefs, put a plea into their lips equally plaufible with that of Mr. W's. objector. Judas, in particular,

particular, might have been furnifhed with a fhield from your armory to repel the threatenings of his mafter. The traitor, while fitting at table with him, was told, it had been *good for him not to have been born:* but inftructed by your divinity, he might have replied, ' It is plainly repugnant to ' the juftice of God, that the gift of exift- ' ence to any of his intelligent creatures ' fhould be upon the whole a curfe *.'

Here, Sir, at prefent I leave you advo- cating the caufe of the ungodly; an employ- ment which will affuredly be of fhort dura- tion, as the day draweth nigh in which every mouth will be ftopped, and all the world become guilty before God!

I am yours, &c.

---

* Review, p. 14.

The Quantum of Moral Evil.

REV. SIR,

I NOW proceed to examine your second objection, *If there be a preponderance of evil in the world, malignity is imputable to the Creator ** : or, as you elfewhere exprefs it, ' If vice and mifery' preponderate ' in the ' world, we muft conclude that the Maker ' of the world, whofe character we learn ' only from his works, is a weak, or a ma-' lignant Being †.'

Whether *mifery* preponderate in the world is no part of our controverfy; and whether weaknefs be afcribed to God by our fyftem, or by that which reprefents him as introducing and permitting evil ' be-' caufe it is unavoidable ‡,' let the Reader judge. I confine my enquiry to the charge of *malignity* which you, Sir, on the fuppofition of the preponderance of evil in this

---

* Review, p. 32.   † Ibid. p. 13.   ‡ Ibid. p. 12.

world,

world, have had the temerity to exhibit a-
gainſt the Deity. And here I obſerve,

1. If the *quantum* of moral evil be ſuppoſed to affect the divine character, ſo muſt
its *exiſtence*, in a proportionate degree. Now
as we both admit this, both our ſyſtems
muſt be affected by it, though unequally. If
my ſyſtem be affected by the exiſtence of
evil, it muſt be on account of that exiſtence
being chargeable on the Deity: but if this
be chargeable on Deity, then is your ſyſtem
alſo proportionably affected by it. That is,
if my ſyſtem repreſent the divine Being as
malignant, (I ſpeak with reverence) ſo muſt
yours, though in an inferior degree. The
vine that produces noxious grapes is bad,
whether they be few or many; becauſe it is
not from the quantity, but the quality of the
fruit, that the tree is characteriſed.

Here your maxim ſhould be recollected,
' that one vice ſtamps a character vicious,
' while a thouſand virtues will not atone for
' one immoral habit.' Will not this apply
to the Supreme Being equally as to his creatures? If he be the author of evil in *any*
degree ſo as to affect his moral character,
that character is ruined; he muſt be an evil

or malignant Being : but if the exiftence of evil do not affect his character, neither can its proportionate quantity : for this plain reafon, that if God be not anfwerable for the exiftence of evil *at all*, he cannot be anfwerable for the exifting *quantum*.

Your reafoning, as I have already remarked, proceeds upon the fuppofition that God is fo concerned in the exiftence of moral evil, that himfelf, rather than the finner, is *accountable* for it. In fhort, you feem to confider it as a kind of medical potion, a degree of which may be falutary, and fo might be given from benevolence; but a larger degree poifonous and fatal, and fo indicative of a malignant defign in adminiftering it. But is there nothing fallacious in this way of ftating the queftion? Can any degree of moral evil, in itfelf, be really *good?* Alas ! Sir, inftead of refembling the ufeful poifons of the *Materia Medica*, fin is rather like the poifon of the afp, or of a rabid animal, the fmalleft proportion of which is dangerous, if not fatal.—Did the Creator really prefcribe this deadly potion ? Ah no! it is ' the abominable thing which his foul ' hateth.'—Is man as innocent and blamelefs

lefs in drinking this forbidden draught as in following the friendly recipe of the phyfician? This you certainly cannot fuppofe, or why feel indignant toward the wretch that defames or injures you, and not rather apologize for him as impelled by philofophical neceflity? But if you cannot fet down to the account of his Maker the evil treatment of a fellow-creature, you have no reafon to believe that the Creator himfelf will thus excufe fin, or confider the finner as the paffive inftrument of his own will.

2. Allowing the exiftence of a preponderance of evil to reflect difhonour on the divine character, it muft bo on the fuppofition of that preponderance being *univerfal* and *perpetual*, neither of which can be admitted. If *this* world lieth in wickednefs, it does not follow that the cafe is the fame with the whole creation. Indeed, there is the cleareft evidence to the contrary. For, to fay nothing here of thofe parts of the creation of which revelation is filent, we are informed of a very numerous order (or rather orders) of intelligent beings, who have kept their firft eftate uncontaminated by moral evil; and who inhabit a world where

‘ nothing

' nothing that defileth fhall in anywife en-
' ter in.' Neither is the preponderance of
evil in the prefent world any proof that it
always will prevail here. We are taught in
various paffages of the facred writings, to
expect a long, a happy period, a millenium,
a golden age, when the ballance will be
turned, and the earth be filled with peace
and righteoufnefs. And when the great in-
creafe of mankind during that period, un-
diminifhed by intemperance, war, oppref-
fion, or artificial fcarcity, is duly confidered ;
together with the number of dying infants
(equal to half the fpecies) of whofe falvation
I have elfewhere given the reafons of my confidence *, we have a grand majority of the
human race among the faved—' An innu-
' merable multitude which no man can
' number.'

Part of this reafoning you appear to have
anticipated, and reply, that it is ' prepof-
' terous' to argue, ' That although evil
' prevails in this diftrict of the univerfe,
' good may greatly preponderate upon the
' whole. This is nothing more than an ap-

* Infant falvation. An Effay.

' peal

‘ peal from fact to gratuitous fuppofition.
‘ We can only reafon from what we know.
‘ If evil prevails as far as our obfervation
‘ extends, we can have no reafon to believe
‘ that it does not prevail in the fame pro-
‘ portion through the univerfe. Revelation
‘ itfelf could not prove the contrary; for if
‘ God be a malignant Being, How can we
‘ know that he does not take pleafure in de-
‘ ceiving his creatures? What ground have
‘ we for depending upon his veracity * ?.’

Am I reading Mr. Belfham, or Thomas
Paine? Since I had the honour of reviewing
The Age of Reafon, I do not recollect to
have met with a paffage fo replete with infidelity and fophiftry.

‘ *We can only reafon*, (you fay) *from what
‘ we know, and that from our own obfer-
‘ vation.*’ The fcriptures then contain no
data on which we can place any reliance.
But, if fo, the ancient Hebrews, who ‘ re-
‘ ceived the promifes, were perfuaded of
‘ them, and embraced them,’ muft, on your
principles, have had no reafon for their
confidence. And how is it that you believe

* Review, p. 33, 34.

in

in a future refurrection? I prefume that nothing of this kind has come within the fphere of your obfervation. Reafon, indeed, arguing from the moral perfections of Deity, compared with the unequal diftribution of rewards and punifhments in the prefent life, renders it probable ; but revelation alone affirms it. Revelation, however, according to your principle of reafoning, cannot prove this, becaufe, without a future ftate we cannot vindicate the divine juftice ; and if God be unjuft (I fpeak with reverence), how can we be affured of his veracity ?

Now, fuppofing the prevalence of evil in this world, and affuming its prevalence univerfally, you are confident the Deity muft be a malignant being. Muft, then, the Deity be arraigned at the bar of his own creatures as a malignant Being, becaufe they cannot account for fome circumftances in his providence ? Muft human wifdom be made the ftandard of divine perfection ? Prefumptious worm ! is this thy reverence to thy Creator, to pronounce his character malignant, becaufe thou and the crawling tenants of thy mole-hill are depraved ?—For my

part,

part, Sir, if I knew nothing of a better world, I should think it criminal temerity to accuse my Maker : but as I know

‘ There is another and a better world,’

Temerity would be too weak a term to describe my folly. As well may the Arabian infer that all the earth is desert, or the inhabitant of the Poles, that the whole globe is covered with ice and perpetual snows, as we conclude, in the narrow view we have from this little corner of the creation, that all other worlds must resemble ours. In fact, every argument from analogy or observation leads to a conclusion directly opposite. No two spots of this terraqueous globe— no two plants, or animals, are perfectly alike. If we raise our eyes to the celestial worlds, we discern the same variety. All the planets of our system vary in their size, distance from the central luminary, and in their periodical revolutions. Their external forms and circumstances are no less dissimilar : some differ in their brilliancy and colour; others in their attendant satellites : Jupiter has his belts, and Saturn has his ring. Thus ‘ one star differs from another star in glory.’

What

What reason have we then to affert that, where every other circumftance differs, the moral character of all worlds muft uniformly be the the fame?

If we receive the authority of revelation the cafe is ftill more clear. The facred writers inform us of ten thoufand times ten thoufand, and thoufands of thoufands, of pure and happy fpirits who attend on the divine prefence, and worfhip before the throne: and, comparing the lights of fcripture and philofophy, it appears probable to me, that the proportion of evil, natural and moral, is to that of good, not greater than this little globe we dwell in, compared with the innumerable worlds that compofe the univerfe. This, I fay, appears probable to me: but, however this may be, it is fufficiently evident that no juft inference can be drawn from the prevalence of evil in this world to its prevalence throughout all the works of God.

There is one point, Sir, which, amidft all this weaknefs and profanenefs, you have rendered clear; namely, your wifh to admit of nothing from the evidence of divine revelation, but what you know without it.

This

This is the plain import of your reafoning;
and wherein this is preferable to the fentiment of Bolingbroke, Hume, or Paine, I
am at a lofs to conceive. Only carry this
principle into effect and you will give up the
refurrection of the dead, and every other
doctrine peculiar to Revelation. And thus,
Sir, you may congratulate yourfelf on having accomplifhed what one of your fellow-
labourers feems to have had in contempla-
tion—' a retreat to the fortreffes of Deifm ;
' a junction with the illuftrious philofophers
' of claffic times *.' Leaving you in fuch
company, you cannot regret that I here
fubfcribe myfelf

Yours, &c.

---

* Wakefield's Examination of the Age of Reafon,
p. 4.

I

LETTER VII.

Of SATAN and a FUTURE PUNISHMENT,

REV. SIR,

BEFORE I quit this gloomy part of my subject, I think myself bound to take some notice of your ' doctrine of a devil and ' his agency,' and of your remarks on future punishment, so far as connected with our subject. Your representation of this arch-enemy of goodness as ' a being of pure ma-' levolence, who is, to every practical pur-' purpose, omniscient and omnipresent *,' is, perhaps, as far from truth as that of the painters and the poets, who dress him with hoofs and horns, and a forked tail ; nor do I find either pleaded for by Mr. Wilberforce, whose notions, if I do not misconceive him, differ not materially from mine.

If you are a materialist, as I suppose, you may smile at me when I talk of a spiritual world and immaterial beings ; however, ri-

* Review, p. 46.

dicule

dicule is not a teſt of truth with me, and though I have no diſpoſition to enter into the controverſy reſpecting ſpiritual exiſtence, I will frankly give my views of this ſubject, and then conſider your objections.

The ſcriptures, as I underſtand them, aſſert the exiſtence of a ſpiritual, as well as of a material world :—that there are innumerable *angels*, ſo called, as *agents*, made uſe of by divine providence in the government of the univerſe :—that a conſiderable number of theſe are fallen, as well as men, from their original ſtate of happineſs and purity : that they are full of miſery and malice, and wiſh to involve mankind in the ſame ſituation as themſelves. The original chief of theſe ſpirits I ſuppoſe to be *Satan*, ſo denominated as the great *adverſary* of mankind ; and, as the name is rather characteriſtic than proper, it may alſo apply to any of his emiſſaries employed in doing miſchief ; and this has occaſioned ſome confuſion among the vulgar, who may have attached to the character of Satan a ſort of omniſcience and omnipreſence, ſuch as you deſcribe.

In vindication of theſe notions you require it to be proved, ‘ firſt, that the ſacred writers

I 2   ‘ *believed*

' *believed* and *taught*' them; and ' fecondly,
' that this doctrine was *communicated* to them
' by *revelation*, and that they were *autho-*
' *rized* to *make it known**.'

One of thefe articles I have no difficulty
in undertaking to prove, namely, that the
facred writers *taught* this doctrine; but
how they came by it, whether they *believed*
it themfelves, or were authorized to teach it,
are, in my opinion, very impertinent enquiries. . When the great God fends meflengers
endued with miraculous powers for their
credentials, furely it is fufficient to demand
our credit, without, in every inftance, quefti-
oning them whence they received their notions, or whether they were commiffioned
to promulgate them. If the apoftles taught
doctrines they did not believe, then were they
hypocrites; if they preached the commandments or traditions of men for the oracles of
God they were deceivers; if they betrayed
fecrets which ought not to have been divulg-
ed, they were weak and foolifh men, not fit
to have been trufted : in all thefe cafes it is
of little confequence *what* they taught. But

* Review, p. 46.

if

if they were faithful and honeſt men, which
you ſeem willing to admit, much more if
they were inſpired, as we aſſert—we may
ſafely believe all they taught, without any of
thoſe improper queſtions with which you
perplex the ſubject. The ſimple queſtion
with me is, Did the ſacred writers teach the
exiſtence of a devil?

Though I conſider not myſelf as called
upon in theſe letters to produce formally,
and at length, the ſcriptures alledged to prove
the affirmative of this queſtion, ſome of
which have been cited by Mr. Wilberforce;
I ſhall, however, adduce thoſe which appear
to me moſt deciſive, and are ſupported by a
great number of corroberating paſſages.

PAUL exhorts the Epheſians * to ' put on
' the whole armour of God,' that they might
be thereby ' able to ſtand againſt the wiles
' of the devil. For (ſays he) we wreſtle not
' againſt fleſh and blood!—*i. e.* againſt human
enemies, ſuch as ourſelves; ' but againſt
' principalities, againſt powers, againſt the
' rulers [or princes] of the darkneſs of this
' world, againſt ſpiritual wickedneſs in high

* Eph. vi. 11---16.

' places,'

' places,'—or rather ' againſt wicked ſpirits
' on high: *'—that is, ' the prince of the
' power of the air', (as he is elſewhere cal-
led†,) and his angels. And again, he recom-
mends, eſpecially ' the ſhield of faith,' as
' able to quench all the fiery darts of the
' wicked [one],' i. e. the temptations of the
devil ‡.

So PETER derives an argument for chriſtian vigilance from the malevolent activity
of this arch-enemy of mankind. ' Be ſober,
' be vigilant; becauſe your adverſary, the
' devil, as a roaring lion, walketh about,
' ſeeking whom he may devour: whom re-
' ſiſt, ſteadfaſt in the faith,' &c. The ſame
apoſtle, ſpeaking alſo of the fallen angels in
general, ſays,—' God ſpared not the angels
' that ſinned, but caſt them down to hell,
' and delivered them into chains of darkneſs,
' to be reſerved unto judgment §. JUDE
expreſſes the ſame idea, in nearly the ſame
words, a little amplified—' The angels which

---

* So the Syriac---Theophylact, Œcumenius, &c.
among the fathers---Grotius, Beza, Le Clerc, Doddridge, and many others, among the moderns.
† Eph. ii. 2.　　‡ 2 Tim. ii. 26.
§ 1 Pet. v. 8, 9. 2 Pet. ii. 4.

' which

' which kept not their firſt eſtate [or princi-
' pality], but left their own habitation, he
' hath reſerved in everlaſting chains, under
' darkneſs, unto the judgment of the great
' day *.'

JOHN refers, perhaps, more frequently to
this hypotheſis than any other of the apoſ-
tles, eſpecially in the book of his Revelation †. But I have quoted paſſages ſufficient to prove that this is the uniform doctrine
of the New Teſtament writers. Should you
ſtill inſiſt upon knowing whence they had
theſe notions, I will endeavour to ſatisfy
you even in this. They had them from their
divine Maſter, who taught them to refer to
diabolical agency moſt of the evils in the
world, either natural or moral, particularly
vice and madneſs. They heard from him
(we may believe) the ſtory of his temptation
in the wilderneſs: they heard him ſpeak of
their grand adverſary, as the *Prince of this
world*, and the great inſtigator of human
miſchiefs, who inſpired the ſcribes and Pha-
riſees with malice, Judas with covetuouſneſs,
and even Peter with improper ſentiments of

* Jude 6.
† 1 John ii. 14. iii. 18. Rev. ii. 13. iii. 9, xx. 2, &c.

falſe

falfe tendernefs for his Mafter *.—It will
be proper now, Sir, to liften to your objections.

1. You fay, ' the exiftence of an evil fpi-
' rit is no where exprefsly taught as a doc-
' trine of Revelation.' I admire the caution
difplayed in this fentence. You do not fimply fay, it is ' not taught;' but not ' *exprefsly*
' taught:' and if even here you fhould be
refuted, you have another referve—' it is not
' taught *as a doctrine of revelation* ;' but only
(I fuppofe) as a private dogma of the writer.
Both thefe infinuations have been I think already fufficiently refuted and expofed.

2. You affure us—' It was unknown to
' the Jews previous to the captivity; but
' was probably borrowed by their learned
' men, at that time from the oriental philo-
' fophy, of which it is well known to have
' conftituted an effential part.' This is faid
on the fuppofition that the Book of Job was
not written till this period—a fuppofition
that appears to me not only gratuitous, but
evidently erroneous; for proof of which I
muft refer however to Bp. Lowth's Lec-

* John viii. 44. xiii. 2. Matt. xvi. 23.

tures,

tures, and Mr. PETERS's Critical Differtation upon Job. But it is not in Job only that
the name and character of *Satan* may be
found. It occurs in other parts of the Old
Teftament. The word in the original properly fignifies an *adverfary,* and in many places
it is thus tranflated *. It is fuppofed to be
ufed, however, as a proper name, both by
David, and the author of the firft book of
Chronicles, as well as by the prophet *Zecha-*
riah †. Bifhop WATSON is of opinion, that
it was originally the proper name of the depraved archangel, and was from thence made
the root of a verb, implying enmity : however, as this verb is certainly *Hebrew,* there
feems no reafon for afcribing the name or
character to a Chaldaic original, as you have
done, after the example of *Voltaire* and
Thomas Paine.

3. You deny, that by the *Prince of*
this World, our Lord intended Satan, and fuppofe his meaning to be, that he ' was about
' to be unjuftly arrefted by the Roman magi-
' ftrate.' Let us examine :—The expreffion

---

* See Num. xxii, 22, 32.—1 Sam. xxix, 4.—2 Sam.
xix, 22.—1 Kings v. 4.—xi, 14, 23, 25.

† Pfalm cix. 6.—1 Chron. xxi. 1.—Zech. iii. 1, 2.

is

is ufed three times by our Lord, according
to his beloved difciple *, and may naturally
be fuppofed to have the like import in them
all. In the firft inftance, a heavenly voice
had been heard in approbation of the Son
of God. But, faid he, this voice was ' not
' for my fake, but for yours '—to fortify you
in the approaching trial of your faith during
my crucifixion and death. ' Now' in this
event ' is the judgment of this world :' now
fhall ' the *Prince of this World* be caft out' of
his dominion. ' And I, when I be lifted up
' from the earth,' upon the crofs, ' will draw
' all men unto me.' The fecond paffage is
cited by you and Mr. Wilberforce, and was
uttered in fimilar circumftances. Jefus had
been fpeaking of his end, and preparing the
minds of his difciples for the event. ' I have
' told you before it cometh to pafs, that when
' it is come to pafs, ye might believe. Here-
' after,' as my fufferings draw nearer, ' I will
' not talk much with you : for the Prince of
' this World cometh, and hath nothing'—or
as fome copies read, ' can find nothing in me.'
—' But that the world may know that I love
' the Father; and as the Father gave me com-

* John xii, 31. xiv. 30. xvi. 11.

mandment

' mandment, fo I do—arife, let us go hence :'
that is, let us go forth to meet the danger,
and prove the readinefs with which I obey
my Father, even unto his laft painful command of ' laying down my life.'

The third paffage relates to the promife of
the Comforter, who was, in confequence of
the death of Chrift, to ' convince,' or rather
' convict the world of fin, of righteoufnefs,
' and of judgment :'—of the latter, ' becaufe
' the Prince of this world is judged.'

'By a comparifon of thefe texts with each
other, and with their refpective contexts,
which I take to be the proper method of criticifm, it appears to me that they are all, to
a certain degree, fynonymous, referring to
the fame event, and to the fame perfon ; of
which, if there can be any queftion, the following circumftance will be fufficient to
decide. In feveral paffages *, the crucifixion
of Chrift is fpoken of as an act of triumph
over Satan and his hofts, and the over-
throw of his empire : By this ' the Prince of
' this world was judged,' condemned, and his
caufe deftroyed ; and it was this that prepar-

* See Col. ii. 15. Heb. ii. 14, &c.

ed

ed the way for the gifts of the Spirit, and the confequent fucceffes of the gofpel. As to the title, it fhould be obferved, that Satan is elfewhere called the god of this world, the prince of the power of the air*, &c.

The above texts in Peter and Jude, however, you apprehend cannot be brought in favour of diabolical agency, becaufe they reprefent the fallen angels, not as ranging at liberty, but as bound in chains. Thefe chains, Sir, you muft be aware are metaphorical, and imply reftraint and confinement only to a certain degree. It is our mercy and our comfort, that the great enemy of our fouls is *chained*; yet to the extent of his chain—fo far as Providence permits—he ranges to and fro' the world ' feeking whom ' he *may* (or *can*) devour †'.

Laftly, our fcheme is unphilofophical. ' Philofophers difcover no *phænomena* which ' countenance the hypothefis of an invifible ' malignant energy;'—neither ' do the fcrip- ' tures, carefully ftudied, and *rightly under-* '*ftood*, authorize any fuch unphilofophical and ' mifchievous opinion.' The former part of

---

* 2 Cor. iv, 14.—Ep. ii, 2. &c.
† Job i. 7.—1 Pet. v, 8.

the.

the fentence may be true enough, if by philofophy we underſtand the modern ſcepticiſm;
and the latter may be admitted with the
change of a word or two: e. g. inſtead of
' rightly underſtood', read ' as underſtood by
' *us*, the rational Chriſtians and philoſophers
' of *the age of reaſon !*'

I ſhould not have thought it neceſſary to
connect with this diſcuſſion, the doctrine of
eternal puniſhment, if you had not drawn it
into the ſphere of obſervation by the following grofs miſrepreſentation. 'The only quef-
' tion (you ſay) is about a plain ſimple fact
' —Can infinite juſtice and goodneſs doom a
' being to *eternal* miſery, for *no other cauſe*,
' but that of not extricating himſelf out of
' the ſtate in which his Creator placed him,
' without any power to act or will * ?'—Not
to infift upon the impropriety of confound-
ing hypotheſis with fact, I am compelled to
ſay this ſtatement is compounded of the grof-
feſt miſrepreſentations poſſible. It is not
fact, nor is it aſſerted by Mr. Wilberforce, or
any other Calviniſtical writer with whom I
am acquainted, that man, even in his preſent
ſtate is ' without any power to act or will;'

* Review, p. 53.

much

much lefs was he fo in ' the ftate in which ' his Creator placed him.'—It is not true, that man ' is doomed to eternal mifery' for ' not *extricating himfelf* out of the ftate in ' which his Creator placed him,' or even the ftate into which he is now fallen; much lefs is it true that he is fo doomed ' for *no other* ' caufe'.

The only caufe of fuffering is fin: and unbelief is only the fource of our mifery fo far as it is criminal. It is true, the fcriptures reprefent unbelief as the great caufe of con-demnation; becaufe it rejects the remedy which God has provided in the gofpel. Our Lord has taught us to confider the Brazen Serpent as typical of himfelf and his falva-tion. Suppofe an Ifraelite ftung with one of the fiery ferpents, and dying with the tor-ture, directed to its brazen Type:—Suppofe this man to be poffeffed of a philofophical genius; and not being able to difcover any ' phænomena which countenance the ' hypothefis,' that the fight of a brazen ferpent could heal the bite of a real one, he turns away from it with as much fcorn as you reject the atonement of the Saviour; he trufts to nature, or to medicine for a cure, and pe-

rifhes

rifhes like a philofopher. Now, Sir, it was the fting of the ferpent which was the primary caufe of this man's death, yet may it alfo be fairly attributed to his rejection of the remedy provided by authority, becaufe all who looked live. Thus our own tranfgreffions are the primary caufe of our condemnation ; yet when a remedy is provided in the gofpel, the rejection of it may be properly confidered as the more immediate caufe :—
' Except ye believe—ye fhall die in your
' fins.'

Still you will object, that we reprefent man under an abfolute inability to believe, which therefore excufes his unbelief. Let me, however, beg you to confider the nature of this inability, that it is not natural, but moral. Either the man is a philofopher and can find no phænomena in nature to countenance the gofpel method of falvation, and therefore *cannot* believe it; or he loves his vices and *cannot* perfuade himfelf to renounce them for the humbling virtues of the gofpel. In fhort, he is a proud man who *cannot* ftoop—a revengeful man who *cannot* forgive—a lafcivious man who *cannot* mortify—or an idle man who *cannot* work ;—fuch are
the

the pleas, and fuch is the inability of finners. Judge you, whether this excufes, or aggravates, their crime.

As to the doctrine of *eternal* punifhment, I am aware of its unpopularity among philofophers ; yet I believe the principal objections to it, arife from mifconception, or from miftaken fentiments of compaffion. Our feelings are not the teft of truth; yet I abhor the idea of arbitary punifhment as much as you can. God originally fixed an indiffoluble connection between fin and pain; and at the fame time endued man, as I conceive, with an immortal foul. None of the perfections of the Deity could bind him to disjoin the connection between fin and its natural confequences; or to revoke the immortality of the finner. Death, it is true, by intervening, produces a temporary fufpenfion of animal fenfation ; but even you cannot confider it as annihilation, without giving up the refurrection.

You allow, that ' in the nature of things, ' mifery is neceffarily connected with vice.*' Let us fuppofe, that God had been pleafed to have punifhed the finner in the prefent

* Review, p. 14.

world,

world, only by fuffering the natural confequences of vice to take place without
mortality :—What then would have been
the iffue ?—Debauchery would have induced immortal difeafe—and one fin, in
many inftances, have plunged the tranfgreffor into perpetual mifery. His character
ruined, muft have expofed him to everlafting
fhame and remorfe; and earth would have
been an hell of eternal punifhment. Now,
as fin is in its nature hardening and progref-
five, the queftion is, fuppofing men to per-
fift for ever in this courfe of fin, whether
the juftice of God require him, either to dif-
folve the original union between fin and forrow, or to terminate their exiftence and their
pain together ?—I think hardly any man
capable of forefeeing confequences, would
maintain the affirmative. Yet, if *juſtice*
require not this, no other attribute can—for
mercy muft be free.

Farther, it is not for us to pronounce upon
the degree of demerit which attaches to moral evil. The facred writers have declared
fin to be ' exceeding finful ;' and that it is ' an
' evil and bitter thing to depart from the
' living God.' And were we in other re-

L. fpects

spects equal to the task, we are too much implicated in the question to decide impartially. Light thoughts of sin, and apologies for vice, may indeed harmonize with the other parts of your scheme; and truly, if moral evil had so little criminality attached to it, as Unitarian writers seem unanimous in supposing, we might well dispense with the doctrines of the atonement, and the divinity of the Saviour.

I do not think it necessary to cite here the various scriptures which denounce endless, or everlasting punishment against sinners finally impenitent. You know, Sir, the Judge himself hath said—' That these shall go into ' everlasting punishment—where the worm ' dieth not, and the fire is not quenched.' I know that you possess a critical talent whereby you can explain *everlasting* to mean temporary; and *endless,* but of short duration. By the same art you can explain away every important fact or doctrine of the Bible; but, Sir, if any human laws had attached to certain crimes a certain fearful punishment; and if the terms to express that punishment were as naturally expressive of death, as those employed in the scriptures on this subject are

of

of endlefs mifery *, we fhould think *that*
criminal might be much better employed,
who, inftead of cherifhing repentance,
and fuing for a pardon, fhould perfuade
himfelf and his fellow-prifoners, that the
fentence would not be literally inflicted—
that it bore fome milder import, and intended merely a temporary chaftifement.

You, Sir, appear to confider the providence of God, in placing his creatures in circumftances fo perilous to their virtue as ours
are in the prefent life, as rendering him accountable, and excufing them; and accordingly plead the injuftice of punifhment fo

---

* The natural and obvious import of the terms ren-
dered eternal and everlafting, ($\alpha\iota\omega\nu\iota o\nu$, &c.) has been
very fully examined by the prefent Dr. Jonathan
Edwards, in his Anfwer to Dr. Chauncey, to which I
therefore refer.
As thefe terms are applied to the mifery of the impenitent, they are greatly ftrengthened by fuch confiderations as thefe, viz. 1. They are the fame that
are applied to the eternal happinefs of the bleffed. 2.
They are explained by other terms which admit of
no equivocation, as " their worm dieth not—they
' never fhall be forgiven—fhall not fee life," &c.
which give thefe words in this connection a peculiar
emphafis.

fevere

fevere as that of endlefs mifery *. But if
God were accountable for the fins of men
upon this principle, it muft not be for part
only, but for the whole ; fince you acknowledge plainly that the whole muft ultimately
be referred to God ;* and this would fet afide
not only the equity of eternal punifhment,
but of punifhment for fin altogether. Thus
inftead of every mouth being ftopped, and
all the world becoming guilty before God,
all men would be furnifhed with a fubftan-
tial plea in arreft of judgment, and in excufe
of punifhment, whether of long or of fhort
duration. And thus the greateft criminal
might appear before the bar of Heaven, and
plead as you have taught him—' I am what
my Creator made me'†; or as Paul exprefles
the plea of the reprobate—' Why doth he
' yet find fault, for who hath refifted his
' will ?' Or, in an immediate addrefs to the
Creator * himfelf—' Why haft thou made
me thus ?' ‡

The above reprefentation of all punifhment as the confequence of fin by an immu-
table and eternal law of nature—or rather of

* Review, p. 41. † Ibid, 33.---‡ Rom. ix. 19, 20.

the

the God of nature,—filences, with me, all complaints of its cruelty or injuſtice; while the doctrine of redemption by the Son of God opens a viſta through the gloom of this ſub- ject, that converts my ſilence into praiſe.— O Sir, if you and I ſhould be the ſubjects of this mercy, we ſhall find ſuch abundant rea- ſon for humility and gratitude as it reſpects ourſelves, as will make us well ſatisfied to leave our fellow ſinners in his hands, and ſay—' Shall not the Judge of all the earth ' do right ?' In this temper I remain,

Your's, &c.

LETTER VIII.

Unitarian Notions of Atonement.

Rev. Sir,

BEFORE we enter on the doctrine of atonement, I shall attempt to wipe away an aspersion on Mr. Wilberforce, and the friends of evangelical truth, for which there appears to me no just occasion. I allude to your charge against us, of representing the 'Father and the Son as distinct beings, of dif- 'ferent, and even *opposite* characters; the Fa- 'ther stern, severe, and inflexible; the Son all 'gentleness and compassion; submitting to 'bear his Father's wrath, and to appease his 'anger, by substituting himself in the stead 'of the sinner*. It is impossible to regard 'these two characters with equal affection, 'and the love of the *imaginary* Christ robs 'the living and true God of his honour and 'homage *.'

* Page 126.

Some

Some parts of this charge appear to me totally untrue, and the reft exaggerated.

1. It is *not true* that we reprefent the Father and Son as *diftinct beings*. On the contrary, Mr. B. knows that the creeds and confeffions of all Trinitarian churches reprefent them as *one being*—as *one God :* according to the Son's declaration, ' I and my Father are *one*.'

Again, it is *not true* that we reprefent them as ' *different* and even *oppofite* characters ;' becaufe we always infift that the Son is ' the *exprefs image* of the Father,' poffeffing the fame divine perfections, both natural and moral ; as well, therefore, may the wax and the feal be fuppofed to bear diffecharacters, as the Father and the Son.

It is *not true*, as this fuppofes and infinuates, that we reprefent the Son's fufferings as the *caufe* of the Father's love. On the contrary, we conftantly maintain that the Father's love and mercy induced him to give his Son. 'God *fo* loved the world that he ' gave his only begotten Son, that whofoever ' believeth in him, fhould not perifh, but ' have everlafting life !'

Laftly. It is *not true* that by honouring the

Son

Son we dishonour the Father; at least, if the Son himself may be believed: for he says that ' the Father judgeth no man; but hath ' committed all judgment unto the Son: ' that all men should honour the Son, even ' as they honour the Father: He that ho- ' noureth not the Son, honoureth not the Fa- ' ther which hath sent him.'

2. That part of the charge is *exaggerated*, which accuses us with ' representing the Fa- ' ther as stern, severe, inflexible; the Son all ' gentleness and compassion.' It is true indeed, that we represent the Deity as

' Full-orb'd, in his whole round of rays complete.'

Nor dare we sacrifice the glory of any of his attributes to advance the others; or reduce them to any human standard of ideal excellence.

We believe that God is equally, (i. e. infinitely) great and good, just and merciful: That he hates sin and is angry at the sinner *; yet is well pleased to display pardoning mercy thro' the atonement he has provided, as I shall have occasion presently to shew. But we do not confine these attri-

* Jer. xliv, 4.---Pf. vii, 11.

butes

butes to the Father, fince, as already hinted,
we believe the Father and Son to be one
God—' the fame in fubftance, equal in
' power and glory.' So far from reprefenting the Son as ' all gentlenefs and com-
' paffion,' we know that ' the Lamb of God'
is alfo ' the Lion of the tribe of Judah ;' and
we look for him a fecond time from heaven,
to take vengeance on his enemies. Thus
Dr. Watts, the writer particularly pointed at,
in his hymns :

> ' His words of prophecy reveal
> ' Eternal counfels, deep defigns;
> ' His grace and *vengeance* fhall fulfil
> ' The peaceful and the *dreadful* lines.*

Thefe hints premifed, we proceed to confider the doctrine of the ATONEMENT.—
This doctrine of the crofs appears as much
foolifhnefs to you, and the philofophers of
this age, as it did to thofe of the firft age
of chriftianity. A circumftance that fhould
make you cautious, left you alfo ftum-
ble at the ftumbling ftone† which is laid in
Zion.

* Hymns xxv. b. 1.---See alfo Hymns xxviii, xxix.---
Pfalm ii. &c. † Rom. ix, 32, 33.

M   In

In opening this part of the controverſy, you give us three different ſchemes of the atonement, affecting to doubt which Mr. Wilberforce would prefer. I call this *affectation*, becauſe, after the attachment Mr. W. had profeſſed to the articles of the church of England, and to the Calviniſtic writers, or even from the expreſſions you quote, I ſhould ſuppoſe you could have no ſuſpicion of his leaning to Arminianiſm; much leſs to the more novel hypotheſis of Dr. Taylor. Yet, as writing a *practical* diſcourſe, and mentioning points of doctrine only incidentally, Mr. W. might not think it neceſſary to ſtate his principles ſyſtematically; but reſted in a general and ſcriptural definition of the nature of Chriſtianity, as ' a ſcheme ' for juſtifying the ungodly by Chriſt's dy- ' ing for them:' a propoſition ſo unexceptionable, that you admit all Chriſtians muſt give it a verbal aſſent, however different may be their ideas reſpecting it.

I might here object to your ſtatement of the *Calviniſtic* doctrine of atonement, as inaccurate and defective; being founded rather on the principles of commercial, than of legiſlative juſtice—upon the idea of ſin being

rather

rather a debt in a literal fenfe than a crime; which idea is oppofed by the moft judicious Calvinifts,* and favoured by the Socinians, who derive therefrom fome of their moft confiderable objections to our hypothefis.

It is true, that fins are called *debts* in fcripture, as well as trefpaffes; but it is fufficiently evident that the term is figurative; for debts, literally fuch, may be paid in kind : But as the man whofe life is forfeited by crimes, is faid to *owe* it to his country, and to the laws; fo we, by our tranfgreffions, become indebted to the divine juftice ; and, if pardoned, owe our falvation to the blood of Chrift, as the price of our redemption.--- Your ftatement of the *Arminian* hypothefis feems equally vague and incorrect, fince it is by no means peculiar to that, as diftinguifh-ed from the Calviniftic, to exhibit ‘ the evil ‘ and demerit of fin, and the difpleafure of ‘ God againft it†.’ On the doctrine of atone-ment many Arminian writers agree with us, to confider it as a divine expedient, whereby a way is opened for the confiftent exercife of

* See Owen on Divine Juftice, ch. xi.---Stilling-fleet's Doctrine of Chrift's fatisfaction, ch. xi. fec. 3-6.

† Review, p. 7.

M 2   mercy,

mercy, in all the methods which fovereign wifdom and goodnefs fhould fee proper.

‘ The death of Jefus (you fay) is fome-
‘ times called a *Propitiation*, becaufe it put
‘ an end to the Mofaic œconomy, and intro-
‘ duced a new and more liberal difpenfa-
‘ tion, under which the Gentiles, who were
‘ before regarded as enemies, are admitted
‘ into a ftate of amity and reconciliation;
‘ that is, into a ftate of privilege fimilar to
‘ the Jews*.’ As you, Sir, profefs yourfelf a friend to critical examination, permit
us to analyfe this extraordinary paffage.

1. The death of Chrift is called a *Propitiation*, ‘ becaufe it put an end to the Mofaic
‘ œconomy;’ the Mofaic œconomy muft
be then a ftate of enmity againft God, or
wherefore fhould its termination be confidered as a propitiation,—that which reftores
peace and amity?—2. It is called a propitiation, becaufe thereby the Gentiles were
admitted to the fame ftate of amity with
the Jews; but the Jews, as appears by the
laft remark, were not in a ftate of amity, but
enmity.—So then this propitiation was fo

* Review, p. 19.

called

called for two contrary reafons; to the Jews it was a propitiation, becaufe it put an *end* to their privileges, together with their œconomy; and to the Gentiles, becaufe it entitled them to fimilar.——But let us proceed.

' It is alfo occafionally called a *Sacrifice,*
' having been the feal of that new covenant
' into which God is pleafed to enter with
' his human offspring, by which a refurrec-
' tion to immortal life and happinefs is pro-
' mifed, without diftinction, to all who are
' truly virtuous.'—Here obferve, 1. The death of Chrift is called a facrifice ' occafi-
' onally'—on how many occafions we fhall fee prefently. 2. It is ' called a facrifice (you
' fay) as having been the feal' of the ' new
' covenant;' but if the death of Chrift be called a facrifice merely becaufe it is a feal, then may every feal of a covenant be called a facrifice; circumcifion, for inftance, which was ' a feal of the righteoufnefs of faith.'
3. This feal is affixed to a covenant of which I can find nothing in the Bible : God's covenant not being made with ' the truly virtu-
' ous,' as you employ that heathenifh phrafe, but with his redeemed people—thofe who
re-

reverence and obey him. 4 What had Jesus to do with a covenant in which he was no party? Could he seal a covenant made, and completely fulfilled, with thousands of these virtuous persons before he existed? Or with thousands unborn at his death, and even yet unborn? If Jesus was but a man, like the other prophets, how did he seal (or confirm) the covenant * more than David, or Isaiah, or Paul, or a thousand others?

Lastly, ‘ Believers in Christ are also said ‘ to have *redemption through his blood,* be- ‘ cause they are released by the christian co- ‘ venant from the yoke of the ceremonial ‘ law, and from the bondage of idolatry.’— But if Jesus be only a man, like ourselves, and his death has no more concern with the salvation of mankind than that of another prophet, in what rational sense can his blood be said to procure a release from Jewish ceremonies, or Gentile idolatries? The former continued near forty years after Christ's decease; and the abolition of the latter might, according to your scheme, with far more propriety, be ascribed to the preaching of Paul than to the death of Jesus.

* Dan. ix, 24, 27.

Thefe

Thefe remarks may fhew the abfurdity of your novel interpretations; but my grand objections are yet behind, and muft be re- ferved for fubfequent Letters, when they will appear in the form of arguments in favour of the Atonement.—At prefent, I would only add, that another objection of great weight with me againft thefe interpretations is, that they have no proper reference to the moral ftate of mankind; nor to that deliverance from guilt and punifhment, which is the grand object of Chrift's redemption, and the hope and confidence of your

Servant for the Truth's fake, &c.

LETTER IX.

The Origin and Design of Sacrifices.

Rev. Sir,

THE origin of facrifices is a fubject of too much extent and difficulty to be fully inveftigated in this place. I may be permitted to remark, however, that the idea of propitiating the Deity by bloody offerings, is fo far from being dictated by mere reafon, that the wifeft heathens generally defpifed and condemned it; as well they might, knowing nothing of their divine appointment and defign: yet the practice is fo ancient, and obtained to fuch an extent, that it is difficult to account for its origin fatisfactorily, in any other way than from divine Revelation. Taking the book of Genefis for our guide, which I hope you will allow me to quote as the moft ancient and authentic record, we find the practice not only tolerated, but approved of God, in the immediate fon of our firft parents, Abel; and if we may

believe

believe the teſtimony of the author of the epiſtle to the Hebrews, this ſacrifice was offered up in *faith*, and on that account chiefly was accepted. This ſtrongly implies a divine inſtitution, ſince true faith muſt have for its object the revealed will of God; yet, I cannot conceive theſe ſanguinary rites would ever have been adopted by divine wiſdom, or admitted into the Moſaic worſhip, but from their having ſome important typical deſign; eſpecially as I find, that whenever they became mere ceremonies, and were not practiſed from a principle of obedience to the God of Iſrael, and (as I apprehend) with a view to their ultimate and typical deſign, they were always ſpoken of with the utmoſt contempt and abhorrence.*

The ſacrifice of Abel, however, I by no means ſuppoſe to be the firſt, ſince it was offered in the ſecond century of the world. Soon after the fall, we read of our firſt parents being cloathed by God himſelf, or by his order, with coats of ſkins, for which I know but one way of accounting,

* See Iſa. i. 11---15. lxvi. 3. Amos v. 21, &c.

N namely,

namely, that of fuppofing them the fkins of
beafts facrificed *. And, as in that early period
of fociety more muft have been expreffed in
actions than in words, I cannot help think-
ing fomething moral and typical was intended; probably to fhew the infufficiency of
their own righteoufnefs, or acts of penitence;
(properly figured, as fome think, by a girdle of
rough fig-leaves); and point out that robe of
righteoufnefs which he fhould provide, who
was himfelf to be the great facrifice for fin†.
For, whatever may be thought of fuch circumftances in this cold philofophizing age,

* Some wife-acres have, I know, fancied that the
fkins here intended were thofe of our firft parents
themfelves; but whether it is to be fuppofed they
now firft ftept into their fkins; or whether their hides
were tanned upon their backs by the fcorching fun-
beams, is what I am not informed.

† From this circumftance I fuppofe originated,
not only the wearing fkins for cloathing, but efpecially the priefts of Hercules being thus arrayed. You
know alfo, it was cuftomary for thofe who fought for
oracular dreams, or miraculous cures, to fleep on the
fkins of their own facrifices in the temples of Faunus
and Æfculapius: and Lucian, in particular, mentions
a remarkable cuftom of the offerer fquatting on the
fkin of a facrificed fheep, and placing its head upon
his own.

it

it is certain, that in the early ages of mankind all their actions were full of import; though afterward the actions were continued when their defign was loft: and to the multitude, both of Jews and Gentiles, they might appear unmeaning ceremonies.

This appears to me, as it has done to many, the original inftitution of facrifices, though it gives us indeed but a glance at the event. For the events of very ancient hiftory pafs rapidly before us, like the fcenes in fome optical exhibitions; in which only the moft prominent objects can be diftinguifhed, and of them only the moft ftriking features. Suppofing this, however, to be the origin of thefe rights we come naturally to the fubfequent offerings of Abel, Noah, and the Hebrew patriarchs.

It has indeed been objected with a fhew of reafon, that part of the facrifice being generally defigned for food, and animal food not being permitted before the flood, it may therefore be fuppofed, that animals were not flain. But this confequence does not follow; facrifices might be inftituted at the above period, and the circumftance of feeding on

the

the flesh, might be a rite added in subfe-
quent times.

I shall not weary you with tracing the
patriarchal facrifices : permit me, however, to
mention that of Ifaac, to which I conceive our
Lord himfelf alludes, when he fays, ' Abra-
' ham defired to fee my day ; he faw it,
' and was glad*.' This has been fo ingeni-
oufly, and I think fatisfactorily, illuftrated
by Bp. *Warburton* †, that I fhall here only
obferve, that the writer of the epiftle to
the Hebrews reprefents this likewife as an
eminent act of faith, in which the Patriarch
received again his fon, as one alive from the
dead, ' in a figure ‡', or parabolical reprefentation of our redemption by the death and
refurrection of the Son of God ; to whom I
conceive the name of the place JEHOVAH
JIREH, was an allufion, for it was on thefe
mountains that Jerufalem afterwards was
builded, and the Lord was crucified.

But I wifh not to lay any undue ftrefs upon conjectures, however learned or ingeni-

* John viii. 56.
† Divine Legation. Part ii. book vi. fec. 5.
‡ Εν παραβολη Heb. xi. 19.

ous :

ous : I therefore pafs on to what is of more, importance to our fubject; namely, to enquire in what light the Jewifh legiflator reprefented the enjoined facrifices, and how the pious Hebrews themfelves underftood them.

The Hebrew facrifices were of four kinds. 1. The MINCHA, or oblation of flour, cakes, or new corn, as a thank-offering in acknowledgement of the gifts of providence* . 2. *The peace-offering*, which was alfo a free-will offering, was accompanied with a facrifice, of which a part only was to be burned, and the reft eaten†. 3. The *fin-offering*, which, whether for fins of ignorance, or otherwife, was to be accompanied with the fprinkling of the victim's biood before the Lord ‡. 4. The *holocauft*, or whole burnt-offering : of thefe the chief was that offered on the great day of atonement §.

Now on thefe facrifices we may remark,

1. That the object of all the bloody facrifices, and of no other, was to make atonement, and that it was the blood efpecially that made the atonement. ' For it

---

* Lev. vi. 14.   † Lev. vii. 11.
‡ Lev. v. 14. vi. 2.   § Num. xxix. 8.

' is the *blood* that maketh *atonement* for the
' foul *.'

2. That this atonement was made by the
facrifice *bearing the fin* of the offender, and
fuffering for him. Of the culprit, it is faid,
' he fhall put his hand upon the head of the
' burnt-offering; and it fhall be accepted *for*
' him, to make *atonement for* him †.' ‡

---

* Lev. xvii. 11.

† Lev. i. 2---4. See alfo Exod. xxix. throughout---
xxx. ditto---Lev. iv. ditto, &c.

‡ Surely Dr. Prieftley could never have read this
text, or the parallel paffages referred to in the margin,
when he afferted (Familiar Illuftration of certain paffages of Scripture, fec. v.) that ' Sacrifices for fin
' under the law of Mofes are never confidered as
' ftanding in the place of the finner ; but as the peo-
' ple were never to approach the divine prefence upon
' any occafion without *fome offering*, agreeable to the
' ftanding and univerfal cuftom in the Eaft, with re-
' fpect to all fovereigns and great men ; fo no perfon
' after being unclean, could be introduced to the Ta-
' bernacle, or Temple fervice, without an offering
' proper to the occafion.' On the contrary, except
in the cafe of the Mincha, or Meat-offering, we never
read of facrifices under the idea of prefents ; but always
as atonements, ranfoms (or prices of redemption),
and fin-offerings on the head of which the crimes of
the people were confeffed, and to which they were
imputed.

3. That.

3. That in no inftance did thefe atone-ments fet afide the obligations of morality; but in cafes of perfonal injury, reftitution notwithftanding was required to the injured party*. The atonement was to God alone.

4. That no atonement was appointed or admitted in capital cafes, as murder, adultery, &c. becaufe thefe crimes, under that difpen-fation, admitted no pardon; whatever cafes admitted of atonement fuppofed a pardon.

Such was the primary meaning of the fa-crificial language employed in the Mofaic law: let us now enquire—Whether thefe rites had any figurative or typical allufion to the death of Chrift, the chriftian facrifice; and whether the ancient Jews fo underftood them?

That the Mofaic facrifices had a defigned typical allufion to the facrifice of Chrift can-not be doubted, if we admit the divine au-thority of the Epiftle to the Hebrews, great part of which is written to explain thefe al-lufions. The writer of this Epiftle fhews, that whatever was defective in the type was in the antitype complete: and defcribes Chrift

* Lev. vi. 4, 5.

as

as both the prieft and facrifice who ' hath
' made an end of fin by the facrifice of him-
' felf.' The epiftles to the Galatians, the
Ephefians, and the Corinthians, exprefs the
fame doctrine, as we fhall have farther
occafion to obferve as we proceed.

Several circumftances concur to render
fuch an allufion probable. There is nothing
in ceremonies themfelves, much lefs in fan-
guinary rites like thefe, which can be fuppofed acceptable to a wife, holy, and benevolent Deity: it is therefore rational to fuppofe that the God of Ifrael had a farther end
than merely the obfervance of thefe rites
and ceremonies; efpecially as fo great ex-
actnefs was required in all the punctillios of
the fervice.

Farther, it appears in fact, that, from the
beginning, pious facrificers had farther views
than the mere performance of fuch external
fervices. Abel was accepted of God becaufe
he facrificed in faith; Abraham faw the day
of the Mefliah and rejoiced; and in later
times, the cafe is much more clear. I will
inftance in David, in Ifaiah, and in Daniel.

David defcribes the Mefliah as a Prieft

after

after the order of Melchifedec *, that is, a
perpetual prieft. He reprefents God as not
pleafed, nor fatisfied with the Mofaic facrifices; but Meffiah as offering himfelf, according to ancient predictions, in their ftead †.
He reprefents him not only as obeying, but
as fuffering alfo from the wickednefs of men,
and mentions feveral circumftances of his
crucifixion ‡. All thefe paffages are, in the
New Teftament, applied to Jefus Chrift;
and prove that David was not ignorant of
his prieftly character and facrifice.

Ifaiah is ftill clearer on this fubject. He
reprefents Meffiah as offering up his *own*
life and foul as an atonement for finners.
‘ He was wounded for our tranfgreffions, he
‘ was bruifed for our iniquities. The chaf-
‘ tifement of our peace was upon him, and
‘ with his ftripes we are healed. All we
‘ like fheep have gone aftray . . . and the
‘ Lord hath laid on him the iniquities of us
‘ all. . . . . When thou fhalt make his foul
‘ an offering for fin, he fhall fee his feed, he
‘ fhall prolong his days, and the pleafure of
‘ the Lord fhall profper in his hand. He fhall

* Pfalm, cx. 4.   † Ib. xl. 6, 7,   ‡ Ib. xxii.   lxix.

O   ‘ fee

' fee of the travel of his foul and be fatisfi-
' ed : by his knowledge fhall my righteous
' fervant juftify many : for he fhall bear
' their iniquities . . . . He poured out his
' foul unto the death : and he was numbered
' with the tranfgreffors, and he bare the
' fins of many, and made interceffion for
' the tranfgreffors*.'

Laftly, *Daniel*, referring to the times and
work of the Meffiah, fays, ' Seventy weeks
' are determined upon thy people, and upon
' thy holy city, to finifh the tranfgreffions,
' and to make an end of fins, and to *make*
' *reconciliation for iniquity*, and to bring in
' everlafting righteoufnefs, and to feal up
' the vifion and prophecy, and to anoint the
' moft holy . . . . . And after threefcore and
' two weeks fhall Meffiah be cut off, but
' not for himfelf. . . . And he fhall confirm
' the covenant with many for one week : and
' in the midft of the week he fhall caufe the
' facrifice and oblation to ceafe,' &c.†

I confefs that in our Lord's time, the Jews
appear, in general, to have loft thefe principles ; and to be, in moft refpects, completely

---

* Ifa. liii. 1—12.   † Dan. ix. 24.—27.

ignorant

ignorant of the true character of the Meſſiah. They had evidently no idea of his ſuffering, and riſing from the dead; yet we know their ſcriptures were full of theſe truths. Wherefore our Lord, when he ſaw the ig-norance of the diſciples he met with on the road to Emmaus, exclaimed, ' O fools, and ' ſlow of heart to believe all that the pro-' phets have ſpoken ! Ought not Chriſt to ' have ſuffered theſe things, and to enter ' into his glory? and beginning at Moses ' and *the Prophets,* he expounded unto them ' all the ſcriptures concerning himſelf*.'

It is, however, ſufficiently clear that the Jews had, and perhaps ſtill have, a general idea that their ritual contained ſome myſtical ſenſe, though they know not how to explain it, and are fearful of giving advantages to the chriſtians. *Joſephus,* for inſtance, makes a kind of philoſophical allegory of the Ta-bernacle and its furniture, which, though ſuf-ficiently fanciful, clearly proves that all theſe things were ſuppoſed to contain a myſtery†. Nor are the more ancient and reſpectable Rabbins hoſtile to theſe ideas. *R. Mena-*

---

* Luke xxiv. 25---27.   † Antiq. lib. iii. cap. 7.

chem

chem for inſtance, ſuppoſes the Moſaic ſacrifices pointed at ' the offering which Mi-
' chael offereth for the ſouls of the juſt *';
though at the ſame time he confeſſes that
for farther knowledge they muſt wait until
' the Spirit from above be poured out upon
' them†.'

As to the *Pagan* ſacrifices, I think it cannot be controverted, that their uniform object was to expiate, to make atonement, or
to procure reconciliation with their Gods,
whom they ſuppoſed to be offended. For
this purpoſe their ſacrifices were accompanied by petitions to that effect, the perſon who
brought the ſacrifices making confeſſion of
his guilt.†

Nor was the circumſtance of one man
dying for another, or for a city, or a people,
at all unuſual among the Heathen. The
Maſſilians were wont to make expiation for
their city, by taking a perſon devoted, im-
precating on his head all the evil to which
the city was liable, and caſting him into the
ſea as a ſacrifice to Neptune, with theſe

---

* Quoted Ainſ. in Lev. i. 2.
† See Danet's Dictionary of Antiq. in *Sacrifice*.

words

words— ' Be thou our expiation*.' So
the *Decii* devoted themselves for the salvation of the Roman army ; and Menœceus,
in obedience to an oracle, devoted himself to
death for the city of Thebes, then in danger of destruction from the Argives.

In the heathen sacrifices many circumstances of similitude to those of the Jews
might easily be traced ; but I shall mention
one only, which is also noticed by Bp. Stillingfleet, who observes, that *Herodotus* gives
this reason why the Egyptians never eat the
head of any living creature, namely ' That
' when they offer up a sacrifice, they make a
' solemn execration upon it, that if any evil
' were to fall upon the persons who sacrifi-
' ced, or upon all Egypt, it might be turn-
' ed upon the head of that beast :' and *Plutarch* adds, that after this solemn execration,
' They cut off the head, and of old, threw
' it into the river, but then [in his time]
' gave it to strangers †.—Here I pause, and
remain

Yours, &c.

---

* Περιψημα ημων γενα, ητοι σωτηρια και απολυτρωσις. ' Be
' thou our *Peripfima*, i.e. our salvation and redemption.'

† Herod. lib. ii. cap. 39. Plutarch de Iside: quoted
Stillingfleet on Christ's Satisfaction, p. 248.

LETTER X.

The Scripture Doctrine of Atonement.

REV. SIR,

BEFORE I proceed any farther with this argument, permit me to propose a few queries.

1. Knowing, as you do, the public prejudices on the doctrine of the atonement, Do you not think it right to avoid any expressions in your writings or discourses which would tend to countenance an opinion you so disapprove?

2. Were you to preach, or write to Jews, or heathen, having the same prejudices, would you not still more carefully avoid countenancing such prejudices?

3. Supposing Paul, Peter, &c. to be men of common sense and prudence, would they not have done the same? Would they not have been careful to avoid expressions which have an evident tendency to nurse people in ignorance or error?

Presuming

Prefuming thefe queries admit of no anfwer but in the affirmative, let us now examine the language of the New Teftament
on this fubject, as addreſſed both to Jews
and Gentiles.

1. Jefus Chrift ‘ gave himfelf an offering,
‘ and a facrifice to God of a fweet-fmelling
‘ favour.*—We are fanctified through the
‘ offering of the bodyof Jefus Chrift once.—
‘ For by one offering he hath perfected for
‘ ever them that are fanctified+.’ On comparing the laft paſſage with the context, it
pears obvious; firft, that the facrifices and
offerings under the old difpenfation were
not in themfelves, or on their own account,
acceptable to God. ‘ Sacrifice and offering
‘ thou wouldft not, for it was not poffible
‘ that the blood of bulls and of goats fhould
‘ take away fins: and farther, that theirexprefs
defign was to point to another and better
facrifice, even that of Chrift himfelf. ‘ Then
‘ I faid, Lo, I come to do thy will, O God.’
He taketh away the firft, ‘ the offerings of
‘ the law,’ that he may eftablifh the fecond—‘ the offering of the body of Jefus

* Eph. v. 2.   + Heb. x. 10, 14.

‘ Chrift

‘ Chriſt once for all.’ ‘ Now once in the end
‘ of the world hath he appeared to put
‘ away ſin by the ſacrifice of himſelf *.’

2. His *blood*, in particular, is called, ‘ the
‘ blood of ſprinkling †,’ alluding to the rite
of ſprinkling the blood of atonement on the
altar : and himſelf is ſaid, as the chriſtian
High Prieſt, to have preſented his own blood
‘ before the preſence of God for us ‡ ;’ yea,
the whole of our redemption is attributed to
the efficacy of his blood; and that, not in a
few, but in a great number of paſſages.||

3. Chriſt is called ‘ the Lamb of God—
‘ a Lamb without ſpot—the Lamb ſlain—
‘. the Lamb which taketh away the ſins of
‘ the world, &c. § and he is particularly
compared to the paſcal lamb.—‘ Chriſt our
paſſover is ſacrificed for us **.’

4. He is ſaid to be the ‘ *propitiation* for
‘ our ſins—a propitiation through faith in his
‘ blood ††,’ which either conveys the idea

---

* Heb. x. 1---10. ix. 22—23.

† Heb. xii. 24. comp. xi. 28.

‡ Heb. ix. 7---14.

|| Eph. ii. 13. 1 Pet. i. 19. 1 John, i. 7. Rev. v. 9. &c.

§ John i. 29. 1 Pet. i. 19. Rev. v. 12. xiii. 8.

** 1 Cor. v. 7.—†† Rom. iii. 25. 1 John ii. 2. iv. 10.

that

that his fufferings were the medium by which the Deity became propitious to guilty creatures, or it has no meaning within the extent of my comprehenfion*. There are indeed two Greek words tranflated by this term *propitiation*, the one ufed by Paul is admitted to fignify, literally, the *mercy-feat*, or propitiatory, which was the cover of the ark; and the fame Hebrew word ufed for this cover, being alfo employed metaphorically to fignify covering by way of pardon and atonement; hence the correfponding Greek word is applied to the facrifice of Chrift. The other word, ufed by John†, unqueftionably fignifies propitiation or atonement, and is applied by the Septuagint to

---

* Ἱλαστήριον in the LXX, anfwers to the Hebrew כפרת *Cappereth*, the *covering* of the ark, which was overlaid with pure gold, whereon was fprinkled the blood of the victim on the great day of atonement.

† Ἱλασμος from Ἱλαομαι to be propitious. There is no pretence that I know, for rendering this, *mercy-feat*. Why then are the two paffages of John paffed over without remark, while that in Romans is infifted upon with a fevere reflection upon Dr. Doddridge and the orthodox? See Mr. B's Review, p. 214.

P   the

the ram of atonement, and the fin-offering of the Jews*.

5. Chrift is declared to have been 'made ' fin,' or a fin-offering ' for us†.' If this be the fenfe, as *Dr. Prieftley* infifts, then he is the anti-type of the Jewifh facrifices, as already obferved; and as the fins of the offerers were imputed to the devoted animal, fo were the fins of men ' made to meet (as the prophet expreffes it,) on the head of the Meffiah, and he was treated as the vileft of finners on that account: and the anti-thefis requires us to explain the other part of the fentence in the fame manner, as im-plying that the righteoufnefs of Chrift is fo imputed to us; that we are treated as righte-ous perfons on his account. I do not mean, however, that his righteoufnefs is imputed to fupply the defects of ours; becaufe I have no idea of our own righteoufnefs being brought into the account at all. But let the paffage, anfwer for itfelf. ' God was in ' Chrift reconciling the world unto himfelf, ' not imputing their trefpaffes unto them;

---

* Numb. v. 8: Ezek. xliv. 27. xlv. 19. See alfo 2 Macc. iii. 33.   † 1 Cor v. 19.-21.

and

' and hath committed unto us the word of
' reconciliation.—For he hath made him
' who knew no fin to be fin for us, that we
' might be made the righteoufnefs of God
' in him.'

6. Chrift is farther faid to ' *bear the fins*
' *of* many—to bear our fins in his own body
' on the tree*,' &c.   It is objected, that to
bear our fins, is ftrictly to *bear away*, or remove them†; and your learned predeceffor,
Dr. Prieftley, who agrees with you in this,
infifts farther ‡, that the phrafe *bearing fin*
is never applied in the Old Teftament but
to the Scape-goat: another inftance, that
great critics are not always the beft textua-
ries.   This inftance, however, may furnifh
us with a moft exact and beautiful illuftration of the fcripture doctrines of imputation
and fubftitution; for the fcape-goat † was
to have all the fins of the congregation laid
upon it, and then to be let go that he ' might
' bear upon him all their iniquities into a
' land not inhabited,' that is, a wildernefs ‖.
It is true, this type was defective, becaufe it

---

* Heb. ix. 28.   1 Pet. iii. 18.

† Review, p. 68.

‡ Prieftley's Familiar Illuftrations, § v.

‖ Lev. xvi. 21, 22.

was

was not flain; whence the introduction of
two goats in the inftitution, one of which
was flain to reprefent the death of Jefus, and
the other fent away, to figure the removal
of the people's fins, into a ftate of perpetual oblivion; it being impoffible to reprefent
both thefe circumftances fully by the fame
animal. You infift, indeed, that this means
' no more than that God, by Jefus Chrift,
' communicates the bleffings of the gofpel
' with equal freedom both to Jews and Gen-
' tiles;' fo 'that the errors and vices of a
' heathen ftate are no longer a bar to the
' exercife of mercy*.' This is admitting
the myftical defign of the Jewifh facrifices,
though it gives a very lame account of them;
viz. a goat was to be fent into the wildernefs with the fins of the *Jews,* in order to
fhew God meant to forgive the fins of the
Gentiles !

That, however, the term bearing fins
under the Old Teftament is not confined to
their *removal,* as Dr. P. pretends, is extremely clear from its being ufed in a connection, in which that fenfe cannot be at

* Review, p. 69.

all

all admitted. I allude to the cafe of a perfon bearing his *own* iniquity *, where it can
mean nothing lefs than being chargeable
with its guilt, and expofed to its punifhment. When, therefore, the Meffiah is faid
to bear the fins of his people, and that in
connection with his fufferings, is it not natural, and even neceffary, to underftand it in the
fenfe of his bearing their guilt, and fuffering
the penalty? not, indeed, that he was guilty,
any otherwife than by imputation.

The only material objection I can recollect
to this, is the manner in which Matthew ap-
plies this expreffion of the prophet (himfelf
took our infirmities †, &c.) But this will
only fhew that Chrift bore our fins in more

---

* See Lev. v. 1. xix. 8. xx. 17. where, for a
man to bear his iniquity, is evidently to be liable to its
confequences; and when fuch an one became fenfible
of his guilt, and repented, it is provided that he
fhould bring a facrifice (if the cafe admitted one),
confefs his guilt over it, (which was accompanied by
the impofition of his hands; See Exod. xxix. 15.
Lev. i. 4. iii. 2. iv. 4, 29, 33, &c.) and with this
facrifice an atonement was to be made, and the finner
no more bare his iniquity, nor was expofed to punifhment;—but wherefore? Becaufe the facrifice had borne
and fuffered for it. † Matt. viii. 7.

refpects

respects than one—He bore them by *sympathy* and kindness, and from that principle removed their painful consequences by his miraculous power. He bore them also by *substitution*, suffering their desert—He bore 'our sins in his own body on the tree *,' and thus removed them away for ever.

Let us, however, advert again to the prophet Isaiah, and allow him to be his own expositor. 'Surely he hath BORN our 'griefs and CARRIED our sorrows; yet we 'did esteem him striken, smitten of God, 'and afflicted. But he was wounded for 'our transgreffions, he was bruised for our 'iniquities; the chastisement of our peace [or as Bp. Lowth renders it—the chastise- 'ment by which our peace was affected] 'was LAID UPON him, and with [or by] 'his stripes we are healed. All we like 'sheep have gone astray: we have turned 'every one to his own away; and the Lord 'hath LAID UPON him the iniquity of us 'all †.'—Again, in ver. 10. 'Yet it pleased 'the Lord to bruise him, he hath put him 'to grief: when thou shalt make his soul

---

* 1 Pet: iii. 18: Isa. liii, 4, &c.

'an

' an offering for fin ;' [Bp. Lowth reads, If
' his foul fhall make (or be made) a propi-
' tiatory facrifice ;] He fhall fee his feed,
' he fhall prolong his days, and the plea-
' fure of the Lord fhall profper in his
' hand. He fhall fee of the travel of his
' foul and fhall be fatisfied : by his know-
' ledge fhall my righteous fervant juftify .
' many, for he fhall BEAR their iniqui-
' ties.—And again, in the laft verfe—He
' BARE the fin of many, and made inter-
' ceffion for the tranfgreffors *.'

Let an impartial enquirer, after weighing
the evidence here produced, fee if he can
fatisfy his confcience in fuppofing the prophet meant any thing fhort of this—that
the Mefliah fhould fuffer in the ftead of finners, and bear the punifhment of their fins.

7. Chrift is faid to have ' redeemed us from
' the curfe of the law, being made a curfe

---

* In the original, (ver. 4. 11, 12.) the prophet has
ufed two verbs as nearly fynonymous; נשא and סבל ;
if there be any difference, it fhould feem (as Mr Parkhurft obferves), the latter is the moft emphatical. See
Ifaiah xlvi. 4. Both are ufually applied to bearing
burdens, and to bearing punifhment, efpecially the
former : See particularly, Prov. xix. 19.

' for

' for us,*' by having fuffered the curfed
death of the crofs on our account; for 'he
' was delivered for our offences, and raifed;
' for our juftification†.' The connexion
in which the firft of thefe paffages is found
affords the cleareft evidence of the doctrine
for which I plead. The apoftle ftates, that
no man can be juftified by the works of the
law, infomuch as no man had perfectly obferved it, but all are obnoxious to the curfe:
thofe, however, who live by faith, he af-
fures us, are redeemed from the curfe by
Chrift himfelf being made a curfe for them.
If this language does not convey the idea,
that Chrift endured *that* curfe to which
tranfgreffors of the law, as fuch, are
expofed, we may for ever defpair of knowing a writer's meaning from his words.

* Gal. iii. 13. A clergyman, who feems fond of writing againft the doctrine of his own church, and the
articles he has folemnly and repeatedly fubfcribed,
tells us, that the *curfe* of a law is not its penalty, but
its *feverity*. ' Juft as, from their feverity, Draco's laws
' are faid to be written in blood.' Ludlam's Six
Effays, Effay 3. A pretty reflexion this for a chriftian divine—to defcribe the laws of heaven as fan-
guinary, and their Author as a tyrant!

† Rom. iv. 25.

As

As Chrift is called our *Redeemer* and our *Ranfom,* fo his blood is faid to be the *price* of our redemption *. For we are not ' re-
' deemed with corruptible things, as filver
' and gold; but with the precious blood of
' Chrift, as of a lamb without fpot or ble-
' mifh.—Ye are not your own; but bought
' with a price,' &c. It is true, indeed, Mofes is called a *redeemer* in one inftance†, but it is merely in the fenfe of a deliverer to the Jews; for neither Mofes, nor any other, is ever faid to have given himfelf a ranfom for them, or as the price of their redempti-on, as Chrift is, in the paffages above cited, and in many others.

9. Jefus is exprefsly faid to fuftain the characters of a *Mediator,* and a *furety* for us. He is the ' MEDIATOR of the new co-venant'—' the Mediator between God and
' men ‡.' Now a mediator is a middle per-fon, who makes peace between parties which are at variance. Such is ' the man Chrift
' Jefus,' and if it be enquired, how he

---

* Job xix. 25. 1 Tim. ii. 6. 1 Pet. i. 18, 19.
1 Cor. vi. 19, 20.

† Acts vii. 35. in the Greek.

‡ Heb. viii. 6. ix. 15. xii. 24. 1 Tim. ii. 5.

Q   made

made peace, the anfwer is ready, from divine authority—it was ' through the blood
' of his crofs *.'—He is the SURETY alfo
of this covenant ✝: which, whatever be the
exact import of the term, implies that he
was to act on the part of finners, for he could
not be a furety on the part of Deity.

Laftly, None of thefe particulars were re-
finements of the apoftles, or the effects of
Jewifh prejudices ; fince Chrift himfelf, from
the commencement of his public miniftry,
uniformly declared, that the one great end
of his coming into the world was to lay
down his life ' for his fheep'— to ' give his
' life a ranfom for many'—to give his flefh
and his blood for the life of men ‡.

Now, Sir, after reading the above quotations, what muft I, what muft any impartial
reader think of the following affertions re-
fpecting the New Teftament ? viz. ' That
' [therein] the death of Jefus is *never* re-
' prefented as an atonement for fin—that
' we are never exhorted to afk any thing of
' God *for the fake of Chrift*—nor is any blef-
' fing ever faid to be granted to us upon

* Col. i. 20.   ✝ Heb. vii. 22.
‡ Matt. xx. 28.   John x. 10, 11.   vi. 51, &c.

' that

' that confideration*.' The moſt charitable
fuppoſition would be that you had not read
the New Teſtament : the fact appears to be,
that you have read it, but under the influence of a fyſtem which entirely veils its
natural and true meaning. Taking this brief
abſtract for the whole of what theſe writers
have ſaid in favour of the doctrine of Chriſt's
atonement, though in truth it is but a ſmall
part, permit me to aſk, what would you
have thought of a teacher in your ſocieties,
who ſhould have thus incautiouſly expreſſed
himſelf in conformity to the prejudices of
Jews and Heathens ? Are there in fact any
writers or preachers of your ſentiments who
thus expreſs themſelves ? Or would you in
reading an author abounding in ſuch forms
of expreſſions, ſuppoſe him to be a Socinian
or a Unitarian ? I ſhould think it were im-
poſſible.

Let me, Sir, on this point be plain ; and
permit me to call upon you to be frank, and
avow your ſentiments. Do not you, and
other Gentlemen of your ſentiments, ſuſpect,
after all the pains you have taken to make

* Review, p. 112.

Q 2   theſe

thefe writers fpeak like Unitarians, that they were really fanatic Calvinifts? That you do, I cannot help inferring, as well from your con-duct in the management of this controverfy, as from my own views of fcripture. While any expreffions appear to you favourable to Unitarian principles, it is well; but when you perceive the current of their writings runs the other way, then you recur to fo-reign and forced criticifm;* I mean, to feek among claffic authors for new and uncom-mon fenfes to words and prepofitions, of which probably the writers never heard. In the next place, various readings and verfions are referred to: and when thefe again fail, as they often will, your laft refort is, to queftion their infpiration and authority. I am now prepared to hear upon the prefent fubject, provided you find, as I think you muft, that the evidence runs ftrong againft you;—I am prepared to hear that thefe good

---

* I beg not to be underftood as objecting to criti-cifm itfelf, but to its abufe, when employed to ftrain paffages clearly on the oppofite fide; or when made the foundation of a fyftem; for I muft fay with Mr. Robinfon, and fome others, ' Woe be to the fyftem ' which *refts* upon it.'

men

men were not at all times infallible ; that
Peter and John certainly were illiterate, and
Paul a man of ſtrong educational prejudices ;
that it is difficult to diſtinguiſh their genuine
writings, and more ſo, what parts of them
were inſpired ; that certainly they were poor
critics and philoſophers ; and that our own
reaſon, and the light of nature, are the ſafeſt
guides. And here I confeſs I ſhall be completely ſilenced : for I do not mean to plead
for ſcripture truths, independent of the authority of ſcripture.

I am, Your's, &c.

LETTER XI.

The Interceſſion of Chriſt.

REV. SIR,

I SHOULD not have thought it neceſſary to introduce this ſubject, but for the following extraordinary paſſages.—' Jeſus is in-
' deed now alive, and, without doubt, em-
' ployed in offices the moſt honourable and
' benevolent : but as we are totally ignorant
' of the place where he reſides, and of the
' occupations in which he is engaged, there
' can be no proper foundation for religious
' addreſſes to him, nor of gratitude for fa-
' vours now received, nor yet of confidence
' in his future interpoſition in our behalf.
' All affections and addreſſes of this nature
' are unauthorized by the Chriſtian revela-
' tion, and are infringments on the preroga-
' tive of God *.'

Had I met with this paſſage in ſome unknown author, I ſhould have regretted his
ignorance of the New Teſtament, and have

* Review, p. 85.

ſuppoſed

suppofed he had feen only fome fragments
of the gofpels; little fhould I have fup-
that fuch a paffage could have been written
by a teacher of chriftianity. Such however appears to be the fact, and may
cure us of wondering at any thing from *rational* divines!

As you make no pretence to infpiration,
permit us to examine, 1. The truth of your
premifes, and 2. The juftnefs of your conclufions.

1. You know not *where* Jefus is; you
feem in as much fufpenfe as Mary was, yet
without her anxiety, when fhe faid, ' They
' have taken away my Lord, and I know
' not where they have laid him.' The
Apoftles and Evangelifts employ a very different language when they fpeak of their
Lord's glory fince his refurrection.—They
tell us, he has ' afcended into heaven—has
' entered into the prefence of God for us—
' is fat down on the right-hand of the Ma-
' jefty on high.'

Should you reply, you admit the refidence of Chrift in heaven, only that you
know not where heaven is—what then? Does
it follow from thence that there can be no
com-

communications with it? I suppose you are as much acquainted with the heaven where Christ resides, as with heaven the abode of God and angels. It was the glory of the primitive christians to hold communion with the celestial world, their conversation was in heaven, their affections were set on things above, their communion was with the Father, and the Son. And if you, Sir, are a total stranger to the like experience, I much fear that you are not only ignorant where heaven is, but not in the way to find it. You know not where Jesus is, and have no expectations from him! You remind me, Sir, of some whose sentiments and language appear to have greatly corresponded with yours—' As for this Moses (said they) we ' wot not what is become of him ; up, make ' us gods that shall go before us.'

But you are equally ignorant of Christ's present employment. An Apostle says, ' He ' is now at the right-hand of God, making ' intercession for us *.' But God, you say, ' has no *right*-hand.' Literally, as a pure spirit, God indeed has *no hand*; but the

* Col. iii. 1. Heb. vii. 25. viii. 1.

right-

right-hand you know is the place of authority and power, Jefus is exalted to the throne
of God. So weak an objection was unworthy of Thomas Paine, what fhall we think
of it from the learned Profeffor of Hackney
College ?——But you proceed—

.This office of interceffion is alfo afcribed to the Lord Jefus in another text *. ‘ He
‘ ever liveth to make interceffion for them.’
The exact import of the phrafe, you think,
it is very difficult to afcertain. ‘ Probably
‘ indeed (you fay) *the writers themfelves an-*
‘ *nexed no very diftinct idea* to it.’ True ; they
were not philofophers, nor rational divines ;
and therefore, it is no wonder they had no
diftinct ideas ; nor is it of much confequence
either what were their ideas, or what their
language, *if* they deferve no more refpect
than you pay them.

As you, however, appear more enlightned
by philofophy, perhaps you may be able to
affix fome diftinct ideas. The word in the
original, rendered *interceffion* †, you inform
us, ‘ expreffes any interference of one perfon
‘ *for*, or *againft* another ;’ fo that for ought

---

* Heb. vii. 25. † Εντυγχανειν.

R. appears,

appears, it may be uncertain from the text whether Jefus interferes either *for* or *againſt* us—this to be fure is a very diſtinct idea! —' Any interference,'—this certainly is a lucid criticiſm!—I believe it is pretty well agreed, that the term *Paracletos*, fignifies a *pleader* in a public court; and this I fuppofe is the general idea here intended ; but what opinion would you form of a Lexico-grapher, who ſhould define *pleading* to be ' any interference' of one perfon either ' for ' or againſt another?'—A definition equally applicable to a *foldier*, and many other pro-feſſions, as to a lawyer.

You are indeed willing to take the fair fide of the queſtion, and to believe that the interceſſion of Jefus is in our favour; yet you are confident, that all ' we can certainly learn ' from the Apoftle's declaration is, that Je-' fus, having been advanced to great dignity ' and felicity, is, by the appointment of God, ' continually employing his renovated and ' improved powers in fome *unknown way* for ' the benefit of his church.' This is the art by which rational Gentlemen get rid of the plain doctrines of fcripture, reduce the faith of the gofpel to fcepticiſm, and tra-
velling

velling ‘ from Dan to Beerſheba,’ find all barren ground !

It is an unhappy circumſtance in your inveſtigation of ſcripture, that your philoſophy always interferes with your theology. Chriſt is in heaven, you muſt admit ; but then the new ſyſtem of aſtronomy comes in your way. If he dwell in ſome other planet or fixed ſtar, ſuppoſing him to be a man, as you do, what connection can he have with our world ? If indeed, as Dr. Prieſtley ſeems to think, he reſides ſomewhere in our atmoſphere, there may be hopes of reaching him by a balloon— the beſt hope that many have of being where Jeſus is !

As to myſelf, I feel it an object of little intereſt where may be the immediate reſi- dence of Chriſt's human nature, while it is united to divinity. Whether the Man Jeſus ſit on the circle (or orbit) of the earth, or dwell in the ſplendour of the ſun, or the glory of the milky way, I believe he is in the immediate preſence of God—‘ ever living ‘ to make interceſſion for us.’

The beſt idea that I can form of the interceſſion of Chriſt, is from the office of the high-prieſt, who, when he entered into the

holy

holy place, fprinkled the blood of atonement before the throne. No form of words was prefcribed upon this occafion (as in blefling the people), and it is not certain that any words were made ufe of; it was ' the blood ' of fprinkling' that interceded.

' Blood has a voice to pierce the fkies,
' *Revenge!* the blood of Abel cries :
' But the dear ftream when Chrift was flain,
' Speaks *peace* as loud from ev'ry vein.'

The reprefentation of Chrift in the Revelation of St. John, feem to intimate that the interceffion of Jefus is of this nature; for there we find him as a lamb that had been flain *; that is, with the mark of his wounds upon him; and it is very obfervable, that when Jefus appeared to Thomas after his refurrection, it was with the marks of all his wounds †.

2. From not knowing precifely where Jefus is, or how he is employed, you deny the propriety of any religious addreffes to him. You feem to fear that, like Baal of old, he may be on a journey—or afleep, and cannot eafily be awaked, and therefore

* Rev. v. 6. &c.   † John xx. 27.

it

it can be of little ufe to worfhip him. Your
inference, however, does not neceffarily refult from your premifes, becaufe the worfhip of Jefus is founded on his union with
Deity. If he be a divine perfon, the local
refidence of his human nature is, in this refpect, of little confequence. If he be *not*,
then indeed his worfhip muft be, as you reprefent it, ' difhonourable to God, injurious
' to rational religion, and, in a ftrict fenfe,
' idolatrous *.'

I am not difpofed to enter into new dif-
cuffions on the Trinitarian controverfy, on
which indeed little novelty can be expected;
but as you have fo repeatedly adverted to the
fubject of chriftian idolatry, I beg leave to
lay before you, as an individual, my apology
for a practice which you fo pointedly condemn.

My reafons then for worfhipping Jefus are
grounded on his union with the Father; a
union whereby he is *one* with him, filling
the fame throne, bearing the fame titles,
participating the fame perfections, doing the
fame works, and receiving the fame incom-
municable honours. But it is of the laft par-

* Review, p. 130.

ticular

ticular only that I fhall here offer evidence, and that in the briefeft manner poffible *.

1. It is generally admitted by Arian, as well as Trinitarian writers, that Jefus Chrift appeared under an angelic form to feveral of the patriarchs; now in fome, at leaft, of thefe inftances, I obferve that he received divine honours†.

Many writers attempt to account for the adoration here fpoken of from the eaftern cuftom of proftration to fuperiors: but this argument is not founded on proftration only. He to whom Abraham bowed is ftiled JE-HOVAH, and fpeaks under that character. Jofhua is commanded to put off his fhoes; and Gideon offered facrifice (as it fhould feem ‡,) to the angel that appeared to him. Are thefe inftances of civil refpect only?— Equally vain is it to recur to the idea of re-prefentation. Ambaffadors never fpeak of

---

* To prevent the charge of plagiarifm, it may be neceffary to obferve, that the following remarks are copied, with fome additions, from two letters I wrote in the Proteftant Diffenters Mag. for Auguft 1796, and Jan. 1797.

† See Gen. xviii. Jofhua v. 13—15. Judges vi. 11---24. ‡ Judges vi. 17, &c.

their

their mafter in the firft perfon. What would
you, Sir, think of our minifter at Vienna,
if he were to tell the Emperor of Germany,
' I am the king of Great Britain ?' Or of the
Turkifh Ambaffador at our court, were he to
fay, ' I am the Grand Signior ?'

2. At his incarnation, Jefus was worfhipped
in the manger (among others) by the philofophic Magi *, and (according to divine in-
junction), by the holy angels, ' Let all the
angels of God worfhip him †.'

3. During the courfe of his miniftry, he
was not only adored by the multitudes he
cured ‡, but alfo by his difciples § ; and never
refufed fuch honours, nor reproved the worfhippers ; but on the contrary, commended
their faith and conduct, as in the inftance of
the woman of Canaan ‖.

4. At, and after his refurrection, he was
worfhipped by his apoftles and difciples **,
and particularly by incredulous Thomas,
who confeffed him as his Lord and his
God ††.

---

* Matt. ii. 11.   † Heb. i. 6.
‡ Matt. viii. 2; ix. 18, &c.   § Luke v. 8.
‖ Matt. xv. 22---3.   ** Matt. xxviii. 9--17.
Luke xxiv. 52.   †† John xx. 28.

5. Paul

5. Paul repeatedly, and without fcruple, prayed to him in the moft clear and indifputable terms *. John worfhipped him in his divine vifions +; and Stephen died in the very act of adoration, at the fame time being filled with the Holy Ghoft ‡.

6. In the book of the Revelation, we have the whole company of heaven, and univerfal nature, in the moft humble and fervent manner, adoring him in the fame terms and manner as his heavenly Father ‖.

7. We have the exprefs command of the Father to worfhip Jefus, and we are alfo told, that no honours paid to himfelf will be accepted, which are not, in like manner, paid to the Son alfo; and thus our very falvation is made dependent on it. ' He that honoureth not the Son, honoureth not the Father §.'

8. It was not only the practice of the primitive chriftians to worfhip their divine Mafter, but this was their peculiar characteriftic. They were fuch as ' called upon

---

* 2 Cor. xii. 8, 9.   + Rev. i. 17.

‡ Acts vii. 55---60.   ‖ Rev. v. 8---14

§ John v. 22, 23.

' the

' the name of the Lord Jefus *;' and *Pliny,*
defcribing them to the emperor Trajan,
fays, they met on a certain ftated day, before
it was light, and ' fung hymns to Chrift as to
' a God†.' Juftin Martyr declares,' The true
' God, the Father, the Son, and the Spirit,
' we worfhip and adore ‡.' Mr. R. Robinfon fays, ' However the ancients defcribed the
' nature of Jefus Chrift in their creeds,
' *worfhip him they certainly did* ‖ .'

9. The great mafs of fimple and pious
chriftians, of learned and ufeful minifters,
in all ages (our opponents themfelves being
judges), have been worfhippers of Jefus
Chrift, and many of them have even quit-
ted the world happily and triumphantly in
calling upon his name.

10. And laftly, I will add, that the contrary fuppofition, that Chrift ought not to
be worfhipped, charges the whole chriftian
church with idolatry, and makes void the
promife of the Spirit to lead believers into
all truth.

---

* Acts ix. 14. 21. Rom. x. 9. 13.
† Pliny's Epiftles, b. x. epift. 97.
‡ 2d. Apology.
‖ Plea for Chrift's Divinity, p. 46.

S   After

After the above proofs, I confefs myfelf at a lofs to know what reafon you can have for afferting, that ' the holy and humble Jefus ' would *doubtlefs have rejeĉted with abhor-* ' *rence* thofe divine honours, which his mif-- ' taken followers in latter ages have afcrib- ' ed to him, had they been addreffed to ' him previous to his departure from the ' world*.' One thing, however, ftrikes me very forcibly ; namely, that it is impoffible to reconcile the conduĉt of Jefus, in receiv- ing divine honours, with his ' holy and ' humble' charaĉter, upon the fuppofition of his being a man only like ourfelves. When the heathen miftook Paul and Barna- bas for deities, with what earneftnefs did they reftrain them from idolatry? when John pof- trated himfelf before the angel that appear- ed to him, he immediately forbade him : ' See ' thou do it not, for I am thy fellow-fer- ' vant.' But Jefus, as we have feen, did not reprove his worfhippers, but commended them. And when we hear him call himfelf the Son of God—declare God to be in a pe- culiar fenfe his Father, and himfelf one with him ;—that he doth the fame works, and is

* Review, p. 168.

entitled

entitled to the fame honours with the Father; it is impoffible to believe, but that he muft truly be a divine perfon, or a vainglorious impoftor. So effential is the doctrine of our Lord's divinity, even to the vindication of his moral character! Before, therefore, you, Sir, oppofe farther this important truth, it might be well to confider, whether you do not thereby virtually give up chriftianity itfelf.

I remain yours, &c.

LETTER XII.

Terms of Acceptance with God.

REV. SIR,

I Perfectly agree with you, that 'there is
'nothing in the whole compass of religion
'and morals, of greater importance to be
'distinctly known than the terms of accept-
'ance with God; or in other words, the
'means which God has appointed for the
'attainment of our ultimate happiness.
'And these are so explicitly revealed in the
'scriptures both of the Old and New Tes-
'tament, that no person of common under-
'standing, who reads them attentively, and
'without prejudice, can fall into any mate-
'rial error upon this subject *.' Thus far
we coincide, but when you add, 'the prac-
'tice of virtue is always represented as the
'*only means* of attaining happiness, both here
'and hereafter †;' we divide immediately.

* Review 104.　　　† Ib.

Let

Let me firſt attend to your arguments, and then propoſe mine.

You quote ſeveral paſſages which en-join men ' to fear God, to do juſtly, to ' love mercy,' &c. and then triumphantly add, ' Theſe are the *clear* and unequivocal ' terms of ſalvation both under the old diſ-' penſation and the new *.' But, in order to make your concluſion valid, you know it ought to ariſe naturally from your pre-miſes. It is true enough, and we all admit, that the ſcriptures enforce the principles of morality and good works; but it does not follow that they make theſe ' the terms ' of ſalvation.' And I cannot help think-ing it a little remarkable, that you ſhould bring ſo many texts to prove what nobody will diſpute, and not one to prove the point at iſſue, i. e. whether theſe be the terms of ſalvation. There is, however, perhaps a better reaſon for this than for moſt parts of your work—there are no ſuch texts to be produced : for, whenever ' the terms of ſal-

---

* Review, p. 105. The laſt ſentence is marked with inverted commas, as if a quotation from ſcripture alſo ; but this, I ſuppoſe, to be an error of the preſs, and not deſigned.

' vation,'

‘ vation,’ as you call them, are named, they appear to be very different, as I shall shew immediately; only I must here premise, that I use this expression, ‘ terms of salvation,’ not for any meritorious cause, as it has been sometimes taken; but, as you have explained it, for ‘ the means which God ‘ has appointed for the attainment of our ‘ ultimate happiness.’

Here you anticipate what I should naturally remark, that the apostles ‘ insist much ‘ on faith in Christ,’ and you admit that they do this ‘ with great propriety;’—but wherefore ? ‘ because their exhortations were ‘ usually addressed to unbelieving Jews, or ‘ to heathen idolaters.’ But you add, ‘ those ‘ who already professed christianity are en- ‘ joined, *not to believe*, but to act consistent- ‘ ly with their profession, and to be “ care- “ ful to maintain good works *.” If this remark mean only that believers are not called upon to commence anew the life of faith after it is once begun, it may be true; but it is trifling, and nothing to the purpose: if it mean that the christian has no

---

* Review, p. 103.

farther

farther ufe for faith after he has once believed, it is clearly a great and dangerous
miftake; for the infpired writers conftantly
reprefent faith as the grand principle of holinefs, obedience, and eternal life. ‘ I am
‘ crucified with Chrift (faith Paul), never-
‘ thelefs I live; yet not I, but Chrift liveth
‘ in me: and the life which I now live in
‘ the flefh, I live by the FAITH of the Son
‘ of God, who loved me, and gave himfelf
‘ for me *.’—He prays for the converted
Ephefians, that Chrift might ‘ dwell in
‘ their hearts by *faith* †;’ and he exhorts
Timothy to ‘ fight the good fight of *faith* ‡.’
And you know that both Teftaments reprefent the chriftian life as a life of faith ‖ ;
and afcribe to this principle all the virtues
and good works of chriftians. John fays
exprefsly, ‘ This is his command, that we
‘ [who do thofe things that are pleafing in
‘ his fight] fhould believe on the name of
‘ his Son Jefus Chrift:’ and again, ‘ Thefe
‘ things have I written to you that BELIEVE
‘ on the name of the Son of God; that ye

* Gal. ii. 20.   † Eph. iii. 17.
‡ 1 Tim. vi. 12.   ‖ Heb. x. 38.

‘ may

' may know that ye have eternal life, and
' *that ye may believe* on the name of the
' Son of God *.' So that the apostles ' in-
' sist much on faith ;' not only to unbelievers,
but to believers more especially, to whom
all the Epistles are addressed.

But our inquiry leads directly to the subject of justification, and the grand question
is, Whether by works or faith a man is
justified ? And here, if Paul may be admitted to give the answer, this cannot remain long undecided ; for upon a full con-
sideration of the subject, in his epistle to the
Romans, he concludes ' That a man is jus-
' tified by faith, without the deeds of the
' law †.' He farther shews that this was
not peculiar to the new dispensation ; but
that Abraham himself was thus justified, as
it is written, ' Abraham believed God, and
' it was imputed unto him for righteouf-
' nefs.' The like is to be inferred of David,
who ' describeth the blessedness of the man
' unto whom God imputeth righteousness
' without works.'

We have been told indeed by some, that
the works here intended are ceremonial,

---

* 1 John iii. 23. and v. 13.   † Rom. iii. 28.

and not moral, and that this doctrine refpects the Jews only. But nothing can be
more oppofite than this to the whole tenor
of the apoftle's argument; who proves, in
the firft inftance, that all men, both Jews
and Gentiles, are finners and alike under condemnation. It is equally contrary to his
reafon, that no flefh might glory before God;
fince moral righteoufnefs certainly gives
more room to boaft than that which is merely ceremonial. Befides, if his argument refpected the Jews only, why addrefs this fubject to the Romans?

James declares, that ' by works a man is
' juftified, and not by faith only,' which, at
firft fight, feems oppofite to Paul's doctrine;
but is fo only in expreffion, a little confideration being fufficient to reconcile them:
James's defign being fimply and evidently to
fhew that the faith by which men are juftified muft be a living, operative faith—' faith
' working by love;' becaufe ' faith without
' works is dead' and ufelefs. In fhort, we are
juftified by faith only; but it muft be a faith
accompanied and evidenced by good works.
Both thefe apoftles bring the cafe of Abraham in illuftration of their principles; but

T   then

then it is to be obferved they refer to different periods and circumftances. Paul fays,
that Abraham, in the firft inftance, was juftified by faith, while yet ' uncircumcifed ;' this
was his juftification in *the fight of God,* and
was without any confideration of his works.
James refers to a period fome years fubfequent to this, when, in the offering up his
fon, he was juftified by works alfo; that is,
his faith was fhewn to be genuine by its
fruits *. Paul therefore refers to the acceptance of a finner; James, to the approbation
of a faint†.

There is another error againft which we
muft be guarded, namely, that of confound-
ing faith with works, or the maintaining
juftification by faith itfelf as a work, operat-
ing in a way of merit, (which totally ener-
vates and contradicts the whole tenor of the
apoftle's argument ;) and faith as a medium
by which we are united to Chrift, and fo
become interefted in his righteoufnefs. This
however is not your miftake : for, though

---

* Rom. iii. 28. James ii. 24.

† The word ' juftification' is ufed in this fenfe.
Matt. xii. 37. 1 Cor. iv. 4.

you afcribe a fufficient efficacy to moral duties, confidered as ' the equitable terms of
' falvation;' yet you difcover no inclination
to magnify the efficacy of faith.

But in what refpect are we juftified by
faith? This perhaps may be better explained
by a familiar illuftration than by the ufe of
metaphyfical definitions and diftinctions. I
have already obferved our Lord makes. the
brazen ferpent a type of himfelf, and of the
Gofpel method of falvation. Behold the
myftic fymbol elevated in the view of all the
congregation! The difeafed Ifraelites direct
their eyes with hope and confidence toward
it, and believing, receive life thereby; but
would any from thence conclude that there
was a merit in the act of looking, or afcribe
the glory of their falvation to themfelves on
that account? Equally unreafonable would
it be to confider faith as a meritorious act, or
caufe of our falvation.—A judicious writer
gives the following apt and familiar illuftration of this fubject.

' It appears (fays he) that free grace is
' the fource of our juftification; the righte-
' oufnefs and atonement of Emmanuel the
' meritorious caufe of it; and that faith is

T 2   ' only

‘ only the recipient of the blefling : and we
‘ are juftified *by his blood*, becaufe by fhed-
‘ ding his blood he completed his obedience
‘ as our furety. Juftification may therefore
‘ be afcribed either to the fource, or to the
‘ meritorious caufe, or to the recipient of it ;
‘ even as a drowning perfon may be faid to
‘ be faved, either by the man on the bank
‘ of the river, or by the rope caft out to him,
‘ or by his hand apprehending the rope : ac-
‘ cording to the different ways in which we
‘ fpeak on the fubject *.’

That the holy exercifes of God’s fervants
have always been acceptable in his fight, is
readily admitted. But in what way? They
can do nothing towards furnifhing a righteoufnefs, that fhall be adequate to the requirements of the law. Were they ever fo pure,
they could not obliterate paft tranfgreffions ;
and being mixed with finful imperfection,
they can never be pleafing in his fight, who
cannot look upon iniquity without abhorrence; nor upon the finner with any favourable acceptance, but thro’ the Mediator. Thus the fcriptures teach us, that fpi-

* Scott’s Effays, No. xi.

ritual

ritual facrifices are no otherwife ' acceptable
' to God,' than ' by Jefus Chrift.†' And
prior to this, it is necefary that the offerers
themfelves fhould be ' accepted in the be-
' loved*'. It was teftified of Enoch that he
pleafed God: from whence the apoftle to the
Hebrews infers that he was a believer, infomuch, as ' without faith it is impoffible to
' pleafe God†:' ' It does not confift (fays an
eminent author), ' with the honour of the
' Majefty of the King of heaven and earth,
' to accept of any thing from a condemned
' malefactor, condemned by the juftice of
' his own holy law, till that condemnation
' be removed‡.'—' The Lord had refpect
' unto Abel . . . . , and to his offering.' The
fcriptures furnifh no examples of acceptable
obedience from perfons in a ftate of unbelief.

The way in which the fcriptures reprefent
us as juftified or accepted of God, is conftantly oppofed to our own works or virtues.
It is by fomething *reckoned, counted,* or *imputed* to us *for righteoufnefs,* as oppofed to a
righteoufnefs which is properly our own. If

---

* 1 Pet. ii. 5. Eph. i. 6. † Heb. xi. 6.
‡ Pref. Edwards's Sermon on Juftification, p. 33.

our own virtue were the ground of our acceptance, that muſt be our righteouſneſs:
but if ſo, there could be no room for *reckoning* or *accounting for righteouſneſs*. We
ſhould not ſay of the children of Abraham,
their circumciſion is *counted* for circumciſion : but if the Gentiles keep the law,
‘ their uncircumciſion is counted for circum-
‘ ciſion.’ It is manifeſt that the term *count*,
in this connexion, denotes a reckoning of
ſomething to a perſon, which does not properly belong to him. And when the apoſtle
ſays, ‘ To him that worketh not, but be-
‘ lieveth on him that juſtifieth the ungodly,
‘ his faith is counted for righteouſneſs *; it
is equally evident, that ſomething is reckoned as belonging to the believer which does
not properly belong to him. In other words,
out of regard to *his* obedience in whom he
believes, he is dealt with as though he were
poſſeſſed of a righteouſneſs adequate to the
requirements of the law ; though, in fact,
he is not ſo, but ſtands condemned by it as
ungodly. Thus Paul writing to Philemon,
ſays, ‘ If he (Oneſimus) hath wronged thee,
‘ or oweth thee ought, put that on mine

* Rom. iv. 5.

‘ account,

' account *, (i. e. impute or reckon it to me †)—' I will repay it.' Here the writer evidently means to place himfelf in the debtor, or offender's place, not as having incurred the debt; but as being willing to become anfwerable for it.

In the Mofaic law we have had occafion to obferve the doctrine of *imputation* as it refpected the Jewifh facrifices. When the perfon who brought the facrifice had confeff-ed his fins over the bullock, or the goat, they became imputed to it, and the animal fuffered the penalty which the finner had deferved. There is a very ftrong illuftration of this in the inftitution of the free-will peace offerings, in which it was ordained, that if any of the flefh was eaten on the third day, contrary to the law, the facrifice fhould not be accepted, neither *imputed* unto him that offered it; but the offerer fhould bear his iniquity, as if he had not offered ‡. From this we clearly afcertain, as indeed I have already proved, that the facrifice was to bear the iniquity of the offerer, and to be imputed to his account; but when the facri-

* Philemon, 18, 19. Τέ]ο εμοι ελλογει.
‡ Lev. vii. 18.

fice

fice was not offered according to the law, then the finner bare his own iniquity—the atonement was not imputed or reckoned to him.

Nor is God's fo dealing with Chrift, or us in him, a capricious, though it be an extraordinary, proceeding. Imputation is accompanied with relation ; fuch a relation as conftitutes a fitnefs in the transfer, and renders its defign fufficiently apparent. In the fufferings of the Saviour we may read the divine difpleafure againft the tranfgreffion of the finner ; and in the juftification of the finner the divine approbation of the obedience of the Saviour. Without relation, and a relation fufficiently manifeft, imputation would not anfwer the end defigned ; but ' God ' fending his own Son in the likenefs of fin- ' ful flefh,' our *fin* is publicly *condemned* in his fufferings ; and his righteoufnefs rewarded in our falvation *.

Whatever is the ground of our acceptance with God, that is it which we ought to plead in our addreffes to him. If Chrift's obedience and fufferings have nothing to do

* Rom. viii. 3. Ifa. liii. 10——12. See alfo Heb. ii. 15---17.

in

in that important affair, it cannot be expected that we fhould be told to approach the
Father in his name, or to afk any blefling
out of refpect to his mediation. The only
name which we can ufe with propriety in
this cafe is our own. You feem to be fully
prepared, Sir, for this confequence; and
make no fcruple to affirm, that ' we are
' never exhorted to afk any thing of God for
' the fake of Chrift; nor is any blefling ever
' faid to be granted to us upon that confi-
' deration *.'

One might almoft be tempted to think,
Sir, that you wrote with a view to ftun and
confound your readers; or that you had for-
gotten that you live in a country where
every perfon has accefs to the fcriptures.
' Never exhorted to afk any thing for the fake
' of Chrift; nor is any blefling ever faid to be
' granted to us upon that confideration !'
Plain Chriftian! who converfeft daily with
the fcriptures, (not to model them to a fyftem; but to learn the will of God, and do
it;) How readeft thou? How haft thou read
the Epiftle to the Ephefians, with the Gofpel

* Review, p. 112.

U   and

and Epiſtles of John ? ' Be ye kind one to
' another, tender hearted, forgiving one a-
' nother, as God, FOR CHRIST'S SAKE,
' hath forgiven you *.—Your ſins are for-
' given you for his NAME'S SAKE.—Bleſſed
' be the God and Father of our Lord Jeſus
' Chriſt, who hath bleſſed us with all ſpiri-
' tual bleſſings in heavenly places *in Chriſt.*
' —*In his name* ſhall the Gentiles truſt.—
' Believing we have life through his *name.*—
' Whoſoever believeth in him ſhall receive
' remiſſion of ſins.—Neither is there ſal-
' vation in any other name under heaven,
' given among men, &c †.'

The expreſſion of granting bleſſings

---

* Eph. i. 3. Mr. Belſham, after Dr. Prieſtley, ob-
ſerves, that this text ſhould be rendered ' even as God
' *in* (or by) Chriſt (ευ Χριτω) has freely forgiven you.'
Thus, indeed, the text literally runs; but that God *in*
Chriſt means no more than ' *in* the goſpel of Chriſt,'
as Dr. P. ſays—or, that God ' has declared *by* Chriſt
the forgiveneſs of ſins,' requires more evidence than
bare aſſertions. The expreſſion of Paul appears to
me clearly parrallel to that of John ; and the pardon
of ſin (ευ) *in* Chriſt, is evidently the ſame as (διχ) by,
or through his name ; or as our tranſlators in one
place expreſs it, ' for his name's ſake.'

† 1 John ii, 12. Eph. i. 3. Matt. xii. 21. John
xx. 31. Acts x. 43. iv. 12.

in

in Chrift's name is too clear and familiar, (one would think) to admit difpute or
doubt*. When Jehovah, under the Old

* Dr. *Prieftley*, indeed, tells us (Familiar Illuftrations, p. 55.) that, ' *in the name of Chrift,*' means as,
or ' in the place of Chrift.---Thus our Lord fays,
' many fhall come in my name, that is, pretending
' to be what I am, the Mefliah; and again, the
' Comforter, whom the Father fhall fend in my
' name, that is, *in my place.*---Praying, therefore,
' *in the name* of Chrift, *may* mean---with the temper
' and difpofition of Chrift.---So alfo, being juftified
' *in the name* of Chrift, *may* fignify our being juftified
' ---in confequence of our having the fame mind that
' was alfo in Chrift.' So it may among rational divines, who can make any thing fignify any thing, or
nothing, as they pleafe; but let us compare a few of
the texts with this interpretation, and with each
other. If in Chrift's name, be in the texts I have
cited, in Chrift's ftead, then the meaning is---Afk
the Father ' in my place, pretending to be what I
' am, the Mefliah.' Or if it mean, ' with the tem-
' per and difpofition of Chrift,' then it is---Afk the
Father ' in my temper and difpofition---Hitherto ye
' have afked nothing *in my temper and difpofition!* Your
' fins are forgiven you for Chrift's temper and difpo-
' fition.'---So, by parity of interpretation, when
under the Old Teftament difpenfation, Jehovah
promifes to forgive or blefs ' for his name's fake,'
' it means, · in, or with, his own temper and dif-
' pofition.'---So much for ' Familiar Illuftrations!'

Teftament

Teftament promifed various bleffings for his *own* name's fake, did not this mean, on *his own account*, without any reference to their merits ? and was not this the fame as for his own glory, for the honour of his divine perfections *? When under the new difpenfation he promifes bleffings in his *Son's name*, does it not certainly mean, on his *Son's account*, for his fake ? What then can be clearer than this promife, ' Whatfoever ' ye fhall afk the Father *in my name*, he ' will give you † ?'—Once more, when our bleffed Lord requires children and difciples to be received *in his name*—houfes and friends, &c. to be forfaken, and fufferings to be endured for his name's fake, is not the fame idea to be preferved ‡ ?

If it be alleged, that though bleffings were allowed to be beftowed for Chrift's fake, the fame is true alfo of fome other eminent characters. Many bleffings were beftowed on Ifrael, for the fake of Abraham and the fathers; and even on other nations who defcended from eminently pious ancef-

---

* See Ifa. xlviii. 9—11. Ezek. xxxvi, 21---23.
† John xvi. 23--26. See alfo chap. xiv. 13, 14. xv. 16.
‡ Mark ix. 37: Matt. xix. 29. Luke xxi. 12.

tors:

tors. To this I reply, if no facrifice, or fervice, be acceptable to God but thro' Jefus
Chrift, Abraham himfelf muft have been
accepted, and his faith rewarded on account
of him in whom he believed. There is,
moreover, an important diftinction to be
made; for though the Jews received, as we
have admitted, many benefits on Abraham's
account, yet they are never faid to be juftified in *his* name ; much lefs to have *re-*
demption through any thing which he did or
fuffered on their account.

Inftead of this fact, however, making a-
gainft the doctrine in queftion, it makes
for it. For it is clear from hence, that it is
not accounted an improper, or unfuitable
thing in the divine adminiftration, to confer
favours on individuals, and even nations, *out*
of refpect to the piety of another to whom they
ftood related. But if this principle be admitted, the falvation of finners, out of refpect to the obedience and fufferings of Chrift,
cannot be objected to as unreafonable. To
this may be added, that every degree of divine
refpect to the obedience of the patriarchs,
was in fact no other than refpect to the obedience of Chrift, in whom they believed,
and

and through whom their obedience, like ours, became acceptable. The light of the moon, which is derived from its looking (as it were) on the face of the fun, is no other than the light of the fun itſelf reflected. But if it be becoming the wiſdom of God to reward the righteouſneſs of his ſervants, and that many ages after their deceaſe, ſo highly (which was only borrowed luſtre) much more may he reward the righteouſneſs of his Son from whence it originated, in the eternal ſalvation of thoſe that believe in him.

From theſe texts I would now adduce a few pertinent obſervations.

1. That the doctrine of *imputed* ſin and righteouſneſs implies no fallacy or miſtake on the part of God. He ſees all things as they are, and cannot be deceived. He does not conſider us as having *perſonally* eaten the forbidden fruit ; nor as having perſonally offered an atonement.

2. That God does not impute ſin or righteouſneſs without a foundation for it in the nature of things. If Adam's ſin be imputed to us, it is on account of our relation to him, as his children and poſterity ; branches

from

from the fame ftock, fuckers from the fame
root. Indeed this doctrine is fo clofely
connected with that of human depravity,
that it appears to me they muft ftand or fall
together. Without admitting Adam to have
been a federal head to his pofterity, I cannot
account for the latter; and admitting this, it
feems neceffarily to follow from that relation, that we muft be involved in his guilt and
punifhment.—It is in like manner we account for the imputation of Chrift's atonement. According to our hypothefis, Chrift
became our federal head and voluntary fubftitute. In that character he fuffered as
our facrifice and fubftitute: ' the Lord cauf-
' ed to meet upon him the iniquities of us
' all.'—In confequence he made atonement
for the tranfgreffors, and brought in an everlafting righteoufnefs, whereby ' the many'
(for whom he fuffered) fhall be juftified.

3. From all thefe inftances in which the
fin and righteoufnefs is imputed, the expreffion evidently means that the party is confidered as guilty or innocent on their account, and confequently condemned or juftified.

4. The

4. The moft accurate idea of the doctrine of imputed righteoufnefs is perhaps to be drawn from the Jewifh facrifices, wherein, as above fhewn, the guilt of the offerer was imputed to the facrifices, and the atonement made imputed to the offerer : and from this it appears to me, that the Old Teftament believers formed their ideas of imputation : and from thence fuch of the New Teftament believers as were Jews, naturally derived theirs.

As to the technical terms fometimes employed by divines on this fubject, I am not concerned to juftify what I have not ufed; and I have endeavoured to conform as clofely as poffible to the language, as well as doctrine of fcripture; but I muft confefs, the complaint fometimes urged againft Calvinifts for their theological terms comes with a very ill grace from Socinian writers, who, on this, and feveral other fubjects, ufe language entirely of their own—or rather borrow that of pagan philofophers and moralifts.

Should you, Sir, after all the evidence adduced, tell me that the language of fcripture is fo highly figurative as to warrant none of my doctrinal conclufions, I fhould

feel

feel myfelf reduced to the fame fituation as if I were difputing with an enthufiaft or a myftic, who, by the arbitary affixion of new ideas to the words of the infpired writers, gets as completely rid of their force as you do by taking all the eftablifhed ideas from them. You might as well tell me the whole of religion is a fable, and that we are loft or faved only metaphorically.

Your's, &c.

X

LETTER XIII.

Of the Doctrine of Divine Influences, and Experimental Religion.

MR. WILBERFORCE * had ftated that
‘ the doctrine of the fanctifying opera-
‘ tions of the Holy Spirit appears to have
‘ met with ftill worfe treatment than that
‘ of love to Chrift.’

Upon this you think proper to obferve,
that Mr. W. himfelf ‘ appears to be under
‘ a confiderable error upon this fubject, for
‘ want of fufficient attention to the *true*
‘ *fenfe* of the fcripture language.’—You proceed: ‘ It is evident to every perfon com-
‘ petently acquainted with facred phrafeolo-
‘ gy, that the *Spirit of God* fometimes fig-
‘ nifies *God himfelf*; and fometimes divine
‘ *infpiration*†.’ So far may be granted.

You add, ‘ The *Holy Spirit ufually means*
‘ the *miraculous* powers communicated to

* View, p. 71.   † Review, p. 76.

‘ the

' the apoftles, by which the chriftian reli-
' gion was confirmed at its firft promulgati-
' on; and Jews and heathens having been
' converted by this impreffive evidence, they
' are faid to be regenerated, renewed, or
' fanctified by the Holy Spirit; that is, re-
' covered from a ftate of heathenifm or Pha-
' rifaifm, which is, in fcripture language,
' a ftate of alienation from God, and en-
' mity to him, into a ftate of *vifible* profef-
' fion and of privilege. Mr. W. and many
' others, underftand that in a *moral* fenfe,
' which the writers intend in a *ceremonial*;
' and apply expreffions indifcriminately to
' all perfons, which the connexion and
' fcope of the paffage limits to the firft con-
' verts from Judaifm and heathenifm†.'

That either you or Mr. W. muft have
greatly miftaken the meaning of the facred
phrafeology is indeed certain; in examining
where the miftake lies, I beg leave to fuggeft the following obfervations.

The whole evidence of your affertions
refts upon your own authority; for, notwithftanding you here oppofe M. W. on fcrip-

* Review, p. 77, comp. p. 16, 17.

tural

tural ground, you have brought no texts to
fupport your affertions: and I am perfuaded
you are too much a friend to free enquiry
to wifh your word to be taken, although
at the fame time it may be unpleafant to
feek for proofs where none are to be found.

So far as I have been able to underftand
the fcriptures, after confiderable attention to
this fubject, proofs numerous and irrefragi-
ble lie directly againft you. Having cited
them at length elfewhere *; I fhall here only
glance at them.

In general, it appears to me, that good men
in all ages, from the patriarchal to the prefent, have believed in the doctrine of divine
influences, and afcribed their religious feelings to this fource. Now, in a point of perfonal experience as this is, where patriarchs
and prophets, fages and philofophers, apoftles, martyrs and reformers, all agree, their
teftimony appears to me decifive; and muft,
I fhould think, have confiderable weight
even with yourfelf.

Not, however, to reft in generals, our
Lord himfelf ftrongly and repeatedly incul-

* Hiftoric Defence of Experimental Religion.
2 vols. 12mo. 1795.

cates

cates this truth, as one of the firſt and moſt important in the chriſtian ſyſtem; and that he chiefly refers not to the miraculous, but moral influences of the Spirit, is evident in his converſation with Nicodemus and the woman of Samaria; in his exhortation to his diſciples to pray for the Holy Spirit, and in his aſſurance, that his heavenly Father would grant this divine bleſſing to all who aſk it.

It were endleſs to quote all the paſſages from the apoſtolic writings which confirm this important doctrine: and to refer all theſe to miraculous powers, would be not only con-cluding without evidence, but againſt it; be-cauſe it appears, that miraculous powers were no evidence of a ſtate of grace or acceptance with God, ſince hypocrites and bad men, as Judas, and other ' workers of iniquity*' poſſeſſed them: and, on the other hand, I ſuppoſe you will hardly contend that the gift of miracles was eſſential to practical chriſtianity; yet this certainly is the caſe as to the Holy Spirit; for, ' if any man have not ' the Spirit of Chriſt he is none of his†.'

---

* Matt. vii. 22, 23.

† Rom. viii. 9. See alſo John iii. 5—8. vi. 44—46. xii. 32, 39, 40.

Again,

Again, It is far from certain that the Jews and heathens who were converted, were converted *generally* by the ' impreffive evidence of miracles.' Certainly many faw them, who were not converted, and many were converted without (as far as we know) fuch evidences. Yea, fome were reproved for infifting on the evidence of miracles;* and a blefling is pronounced on thofe ' who have ' not feen, and have yet believed.†' In fact, the miniftry of the gofpel was the great inftrument of converfion in the firft ages, as in all fucceeding ones; and our own eyes have witneffed the like effects, although the gift of miracles hath long fince ceafed. Indeed, our Lord himfelf has taught us that little is to be expected from the force of miracles where the fcriptures are not believed. ' If ' they believe not Mofes and the Prophets, ' neither will they be perfuaded though one ' fhould arife from the dead.'

Scriptural converfion is not a mere recovery from heathenifm, or pharifaifm to ' a ' ftate of vifible profeffion, and of privilege;' but, in many inftances, a converfion from a

---

* Matt. xii. 39. † John xx. 29.

mere

mere vifible profeffion, which is common to hypocrites and bad men, to a ftate of vital union and communion with God. Thus our Lord taught his difciples, who were neither heathens nor pharifees, the neceffity of their being converted and becoming little children, in order to their admiffion into his kingdom*; and this converfion is uniformly afcribed to the grace of God.

I am aware that it has been faid, this phrafe, ' the GRACE of God,' in fcripture never intends divine *influences* ; but only the divine *favor*. That it often bears the latter fenfe, is freely admitted; but that in many inftances it alfo intends the former, is equally certain. See, for example, the following paffages: ' By the GRACE of God I am ' what I am: and his GRACE which was ' beftowed upon me was not in vain; but I ' laboured more abundantly than they all: ' yet not I, but the GRACE of God which ' was with me.'—' By the GRACE of God ' we have had our converfation in the world, ' and more abundantly to you-ward.'—' We ' do you to wit of the GRACE of God be-

---

* Matt. xviii. 3.

' ftowed

' flowed on the churches of Macedonia.'—
' We defired Titus, that as he had begun,
' fo he would alfo finifh in you the fame
' GRACE alfo, &c.'—' My GRACE is fuf-
' ficient for thee.'—' Grow in GRACE, &c.*'

I do not comprehend what paffages you
particularly refer to, when you charge Mr.
W. and others, with taking thofe fcriptures
in ' a *moral* fenfe which the writers intend
' in a ceremonial.' Are we to go back then
to the carnal ordinances of the Jewifh ritual? Or is chriftianity to be refolved into a
fyftem of religious ceremonies?——As to
what you fay, of our applying to all indifcriminately what the contexts of the paffages
limit to a few, we plead generally, *not guilty*;
but the inftances muft be pointed out before
we can anfwer them particularly.

But you will perhaps ftill plead, that all
fuch divine influences are *unneceffary*. ' It has
' never yet been proved, you fay, that any
' fupernatural influence upon the mind is
' *neceffary* under the divine government; or
' that it has ever exifted, except in a few

---

* 1 Cor. xv. 10. 2 Cor. i. 12. viii. 1, 6, 7.—xii. 9.
2 Pet. iii. 18 See alfo Eph. iv. 29. Heb. iv. 16.

' very

' very extraordinary cafes.' If the evidence
of fcripture might be admitted on the queftion, this would not be a tafk of any difficulty. Our Lord has taught the neceffity of
being born again—of being born of the Spirit; ' for that which is born of the flefh is
' flefh, and that which is born of the Spirit
' is fpirit *.' Which words are evidently
fynonymous with thofe of the great apoftle
of the Gentiles—' They that are after the
' flefh do mind the things of the flefh, and
' they that are after the Spirit the things of
' the Spirit. For to be carnally minded,' or
to mind the things of the flefh ' is death;
' but to be fpiritually minded;' or to mind
the things of the Spirit ' is life and peace.'
' For the carnal mind is enmity againft God;
' for it is not fubject to the law of God,
' neither indeed can be. So then, they that
' are in the flefh CANNOT PLEASE GOD.
' But ye are not in the flefh but in the Spi-
' rit, if fo be that the Spirit of God dwell
' in you. Now if any man have not the
' Spirit of Chrift he is none of his.†'—Again,
' The natural man receiveth not the things

---

* John iii. 6.   † Rom. viii. 5—9.

' of

' of the Spirit of God, for they are foolifh-
' nefs unto him: neither can he know them,
' becaufe they are fpiritually difcerned*.'

If this be true, Sir, I can expect the fcriptures, (clear and decifive as they appear, to
me,) will have little authority with ' philo-
' fophic theifts,' among whom you evidently rank yourfelf : for you fubjoin immediately, ' Every philofophic theift will allow
' that all events are brought to pafs agree-
' ably to the divine foreknowledge, and ac-
' cording to the wife and benevolent coun-
' fels of God. Alfo, that a divine energy
' is actually exerted in every event, accord-
' ing to certain rules which God has pre-
' fcribed to himfelf, few will deny. True
' philofophy, and true religion, lead us to
' fee God in every thing. But that he *ever*,
' much more that he *frequently* deviates
' from his ufual courfe to produce effects
' upon the human mind, which would not
' have refulted from the natural opera-
' tion of general laws, is a fact improbable
' in itfelf, and of which we have no fatis-
' factory evidence, either from experience
' or revelation *.' From this paragraph, I

* 1 Cor. ii. 14.   † Review, p. 78.

fear,

fear, Sir, we have been miftaken in confidering your fyftem as a fort of *half-way
houfe* between chriftianity and infidelity ; for
it feems to bear hard even on the confines of
the latter. Nay, fome 'few' of thefe philofophers, it appears, are *virtually* atheifts, for
they deny the exertion of ' a divine energy'
in providence ; and for the reft, though
they admit this, according to the eftablifhed
laws of nature, yet that God *ever* deviates
therefrom, appears to them, as it does to
you, ' a fact improbable in itfelf, and of
' which we have no fatisfactory evidence.'

This, Sir, may be philofophical *theifm,*
but I hope you will not call it chriftianity.
For if all fupernatural influence on the human mind be *improbable,* and without evidence, we have no room for a divine revelation ; and confequently, none for chriftianity.

It is therefore a very awkward falvo
which you offer for the chriftian writers, and
a very ftrange attempt to bend their evidence
againft themfelves in the paragraph which
follows. In *popular* language, you remark,
' The virtuous affections of virtuous men,
' are with great propriety afcribed to God ;

Y 2   and

' and the pious writers of the fcriptures hav
' often adopted this form of expreffion.
' Whether they themfelves believed in the
' exiftence of frequent fupernatural opera-
' tions upon the mind does not clearly ap-
' pear; and it is certain, that they no where
' affirm that it conftituted any part of their
' commiffion, to teach this extraordinary
' and *improbable* doctrine *.' So then, after
all, it is in vain that I have quoted thefe
authorities—the fcripture writers were only
popular writers at the beft; it it uncertain
whether they believed what they taught—
it is certain, we have no evidence that they
were empowered to preach this doctrine,
therefore, to fpeak in the mildeft terms, in
teaching it they muft have exceeded their
commiffion ! ! !

But the ' Agency which they admitted,'
you fay, ' extends to evil as well as to
' good; " it hardens the heart of Pharoah,"
' as well as " opens that of Lydia;" and
' therefore, it is a general, and not a parti-
' cular influence; confequently the popular
' language of the facred writings by no

* Review, p. 78, 79.

' means

' means authorifes the conclufion, that God
' ever interpofes fupernaturally to produce
' moral effects upon the mind.*' How re-
iterated, Sir, are your attempts to reduce
chriftianity to a level with paganifm ! but
here you go below it; for, though they
afcribed the virtuous actions of good men
to the Deity, I believe they knew better
than to afcribe the vicious actions of bad
men to the fame fource. This is to make
the fame fountain fend forth both fweet
water and bitter. It is true, that the Lord
hardened Pharoah's heart; but it is never
faid that he did this by his Spirit, by his
grace, or by any pofitive agency. No, it
was merely in the courfe of providence—by
permitting his magicians to perform thofe
wonders which ftrengthened his infidelity,
while others probably preffed him with
motives of a political confideration. In this
fenfe only does the Lord harden men's
hearts ; and that, not till they have, as in
the prefent inftance, repeatedly hardened
themfelves againft him. He fealeth down
the eye that fhutteth itfelf againft the light.

* Review, p. 79.

But

But it is otherwife with refpect to good. God is light : and like his faireft material reprefentative, the fun, caufes darknefs only by his abfence ; but they are his *beams* which create the day.

But after all, your grand objection againft this doctrine is, that it is ' unphilofophical.*' On the modern fyftem of materialifm, there may be force in this objection ; for, if we have no immaterial fpirits, certainly they cannot be the fubjects of the Spirit's influence. Still, I fhould fuppofe, that human nature, of whatever it confift, may be exposed to foreign influence ; and if fo, especially to that of the Creator.——The hypothefis of an immaterial and immortal fpirit, I grant, harmonizes better with this, as well as with the other doctrines of revelation : and there can be no difficulty in conceiving of the fupreme Spirit as having accefs to all created intelligences.

This doctrine, though a prominent and effential feature in chriftianity, is by no means peculiar to it ; but has been ufually confidered as equally effential to what is

* Review, 193.

called

called *natural religion*; and fo far from being thought unphilofophical, until within thefe few years, it will be difficult to find a philofopher of any eminence who totally rejected it. Even in the prefent century, Boyle, Locke, Clarke, Addifon, &c. have been among its illuftrious advocates.

Nor can I fee any thing in it unworthy of philofophy, or inconfiftent with reafon. Is it abfurd to fuppofe the Supreme Being has an accefs to the human mind? Or that he influences the mind to piety and virtue? Is it irrational to believe this influence operates upon the underftanding, in giving a clearer view of divine truth? Or upon the affections, enkindling love to God and holinefs, and exciting hatred and averfion to immorality?—But it has been ridiculed: fo has every thing facred. ' It is liable to great ' abufe, and has been productive of very ' pernicious confequences *.' So has the doctrine of infpiration itfelf, and almoft every doctrine of religion, natural and revealed.

Neither is there any ground for pretend-

* Review, p. 79.

ing

ing that this doctrine introduces confufion in the divine government, or perpetuates the age of miracles; becaufe the Spirit of God operates as much according to his eftablifhed laws in the moral world as in the natural; though both may often be infcrutable to us. ' The wind bloweth where it ' lifteth, and thou heareft the found thereof, ' but canft not tell whence it cometh, nor ' whither it goeth : fo is every one that is ' born of the Spirit *.'

It is, however, fimply upon the authority of fcripture that this doctrine muft be fupported; and whatever you might do with the philofophers, you would find it impoffible to deprive us of the fanction of patriarchs, prophets, and apoftles, and efpecially that of Jefus Chrift himfelf, to whofe divine inftruction and compaffion I cordially commend you, remaining,

Yours, &c.

---

* John iii. 8.

LETTER XIV.

Effects and Consequences of the Calviniſtic Syſtem.

REV. SIR,

HAVING thus far attended to the evidences of divine truth, we muſt not conclude theſe Letters without ſome attention to its effects and conſequences, eſpecially as you lay particular ſtreſs on this ar-argument. ' It is from the abſurd and in' jurious conſequences which reſult from ' Mr. Wilberforce's principles that' you ' in' fer their falſehood and impiety;' and you very juſtly obſerve, that ' the natural and ' neceſſary conſequences of principles are the ' ſame, whether the advocates of ſuch prin' ciples are appriſed of them or not, and ' whether they do or do not chuſe to con' template and avow them*.'

Of all conſequences, thoſe of a practical

---

* Review, p. 11.

Z

nature

nature are the moſt important, and it is a very ſerious conſideration indeed, if the practical conſequences or tendencies of Calviniſm be as you repreſent them; ' ſo odious and ' diſguſting*,' that it ſhould ſeem, the only thing which preſerves Calviniſts from being altogether monſters is, that they are inattentive to their own principles, and blind to their moſt neceſſary conſequences. ' The ' truth is,' you ſay ' that Mr. Wilberforce, ' and others, who agree with him, ſeldom ' regard their ſyſtem in a comprehenſive ' view, or purſue their principles to their ' juſt and neceſſary conſequences. Satis- ' ſied with being themſelves in the number ' of the elect and regenerate, they ſee no ' cauſe to complain on their own account, ' and giving themſelves up to joy and grati- ' tude for their perſonal intereſt in the pro- ' miſes of the goſpel, they *feel little concern* ' *for the non-elect maſs of mankind*, doomed ' by the neceſſity of their circumſtances, to ' eternal miſery ; and ſeldom allow them- ' ſelves to enquire how far ſuch a ſtate of ' things is reconcilable to wiſdom, benevo- ' lence, or juſtice †.

* Review, p. 10. † Ibid. p. 11.

Not

Not to notice the mifreprefentation here given of the Calviniftic fyftem, the firft remark I would offer on this paffage will refpect the compliment you have paid to the intelligence and penetration of the Calvinifts —who are, it feems, men of fuch narrow minds and contracted views, that ' they fel- ' dom regard their fyftem in a comprehen- ' five view—feldom allow themfelves to en- ' quire how far fuch a ftate of things is re- ' concilable to wifdom, benevolence, or ' juftice.'—If this remark be intended to apply only to the mafs of profeffing Calvinifts; it may, we prefume, be equally applied to the majority of Unitarians ; for there are in *every* fect few, comparatively, capable of taking a comprehenfive view of their own principles. But if it be intended to apply to Calvinifts univerfally, and exclufively, it may be confidered as a fpecimen of Unitarian candour and liberality, of which many fimilar inftances are not wanting in the work before us.

A fecond natural and neceffary effect of Calviniftic principles is, it fhould appear, that they fo abforb men in their own intereft, as to render them infenfible to the

ftate

state of others. ' Satisfied with being them-
' selves in the number of the elect and re-
' generate . . . . they feel little concern for
' the non-elect mass of mankind.' Affertions
are eafy, and when delivered with confidence, we have often feen them obtain credit,
even though totally unfupported with evidence. But in the prefent inftance, facts
run fo directly and notorioufly contrary to
this ftatement, that I cannot but wonder
even that you, Sir, have ventured to rifk
it; efpecially if you have, as from fome
circumftances I fhould fuppofe, looked into
Mr. Fuller's Letters on the comparative
tendency of ' The Calviniftic and Socinian
' Syftems*.' It is true, Calvinifts do not
feek the falvation of the non-elect *as fuch*;
but as non-election is utterly unknown to
them, it has no influence in retarding the
progrefs of their labours. It is towards men
as finners that their efforts are directed. Not
to enter at large upon this topic, fuffice it
to fay, Pref. *Edwards* was a Calvinift, and
great and wearied were his exertions for the
fouls of men—*David Brainard* was a Cal-

* Letter III,

vinift,

vinift, and he devoted his life for the falvation of a few barbarous heathens—*Whitefield*
was a Calvinift, and he flew backward and
forward from kingdom to kingdom, and
from clime to clime, like ' an angel through
' the midft of heaven,' to preach the everlafting gofpel. Thoufands more might be
enumerated to prove, if neceffary, that Calvinifm does not render, even the moft zeal-
ous of its profeffors, indifferent to the falvation of the mafs of mankind. Let Mr. B.
produce only *one folitary inftance* of like zeal
and compaffion among the whole body of
intelligent and benevolent Unitarians; and
then it may be time enough to reproach the
Calvinifts with their want of zeal and tendernefs to the fouls of men.

Left I fhould be accufed of mifreprefentation it muft be confeffed, that all this felfifh-
nefs and indifference to others is fuppofed
to arife from an excefs of virtue, namely, of
gratitude on our own account. Like a condemned criminal who has received a pardon
from his fovereign, the Calvinift fo gives up
himfelf ' to joy and gratitude' on his own
account as ' feldom to allow himfelf' to ar-

raign

raign the conduct of his judge, either as it
refpects himfelf or his fellow-prifoners. But
then, left we fhould be vain of this virtue,
you take care in your fubfequent pages, to
reprefent even this gratitude as no better
than fulfome adulation to the Son of God,
and grofs idolatary.

3. You reprefent us farther as enemies to
reafon, rational interpretation, and found
criticifm. ' Popular writers teftify their re-
' gard for the fcriptures by afferting or affu-
' ming their plenary infpiration—by calling
' them indifcriminately the word of God; by
' quoting text upon text, without regard to
' connexion, without proper explanation,
' without any allowance for figurative lan-
' guage, or Jewifh phrafeology; and with-
' out any attempt to afcertain the genuine-
' nefs of difputed paflages; citing detached
' fentences as infpired apophthegms; relying
' with full confidence on the received text,
' as though the authority of its editors were
' equal to that of the apoftles, and apparent-
' ly ignorant of all that has been accom-
' plifhed by the indefatigable induftry, and
' penetrating fagacity of modern critics, to
                                        ' correct

' correct the text and to bring it nearer to the
' original ftandard ; equally confiding in the
' authority of the Englifh tranflation ; and an-
' nexing, without hefitation or enquiry, thofe
' fenfes to difputed phrafes which have been
' learned from obfolete articles and creeds*.'

It would be tedious and uninterefting to
analyfe this loofe declamatory charge, but
there is one thing infinuated that efpecially
merits animadverfion ; namely, that rational
criticifm is inimical to the orthodox fyftem,
which is here fuppofed to reft upon corrupt
editions and verfions of the fcripture ; or
why complain of our placing implicit confidence on editors and tranflators? But if
this were true, it muft be fuppofed that thofe
who have paid the moft particular attention
to thefe ftudies, would neceffarily prove
Unitarians or Socinians ; whereas, how contrary this is to the evidence of facts is fufficiently evident from the inftances of Kennicott and Lowth, of Deddridge and of
Gill, and many other critics indefatigable in
their enquiries ; but inftead of quoting thefe,

* Review, p. 27.

I fhall

I fhall offer a fingle extract from a foreign Profeffor, whofe name ranks in the higheft clafs of fcripture critics; I mean the great Michaelis, who, fpeaking of the labours of modern critics, fays, ' It is true, that the ' number of proof paffages in fupport of cer- ' tain doctrines, has been diminifhed by our ' knowledge of the various readings. We ' are certain, for inftance, that 1 John v. 7. ' is a fpurious, paffage; but the doctrine con- ' tained in it is not therefore changed, fince ' it is delivered in other parts of the New ' Teftament. After the moft diligent enqui- ' ry, efpecially by thofe who would banifh ' the divinity of Chrift from the articles of ' our religion, not a *fingle various reading* ' has been difcovered in the two principal ' paffages, John i. 1. and Rom. ix. 5. ; and ' this very doctrine, inftead of being fhaken ' by the collections of Mill and Wetftein, ' has been rendered more certain than ever. ' This is fo ftrongly felt by the modern re- ' formers in Germany, that they begin to ' think lefs favourably of that fpecies of cri- ' ticifm which they at firft fo highly re- ' commended, in hopes of its leading to dif-

coveries

' coveries more fuitable to their maxims,
' than the ancient fyftem *.'

As to the general declamation, it will
weigh light with candid critical enquirers;
if the texts above produced are quoted only
in a detached, popular, or erroneous fenfe,
have the goodnefs not only to fay, but to
prove it; at leaft, produce fome plaufible
arguments in favour of your novel interpretations; for, notwithftanding what you boaft
of the wifdom and judgment of Unitarians,
as ' rational critics,—men of learning and
' enquiry,—enlightned and confiftent chrifti-
' ans,'—I have not found in your Letters one
critical examination of fcripture; but the
whole of your work is a clofe imitation of

---

* Marfh's Michaelis, vol. i. p. 226. In a note on
this paffage, Mr. Marfh obferves, that the author's affertions are not perfectly correct : ' fer John i. 1. in-
' ftead of Θεος the Cod. Steph. η. and Gregory of Nyffa
' have O Θεος ; on the other hand, Rom. ix. 5. fome
' of the fathers have quoted without Θεος.' Thefe va-
riations, however, are too flight to fhake the authority
of thefe texts ; nor do I conceive thefe to be the ' two
principal texts' upon which this doctrine refts : there
are many others, at leaft equally decifive in in its
favour.

A a   that

that popular ſtyle which you ſo pointedly condemn.

4. The moſt curious, if not the moſt criminal part of your charge againſt us is, that of diſhonouring the *ſcriptures* with our belief and confidence, while the wiſe men of your hypotheſis ſhew their veneration for them by their ſuſpicions and doubts—querying, altering, or rejecting texts, chapters, and whole books of ſcripture, as may ſuit their purpoſe.

It would be impertinent to deſcend here to particulars, but there is one paſſage which I cannot help citing as ſufficiently deciſive of your attachment to the ſcriptures. ‘ The ‘ ſcriptures’ you tell us ‘ contain a faithful ‘ and credible account of the *chriſtian doctrine,* ‘ which is the *true word of God:* but they ‘ are not *themſelves* the word of God, nor do ‘ they ever aſſume that title: and it is highly ‘ improper to ſpeak of them as ſuch; as it ‘ leads inattentive readers to ſuppoſe they ‘ were written under a *plenary inſpiration,* to ‘ which they make no pretenſion; and as ‘ ſuch expreſſions expoſe chriſtianity unne- ‘ ceſſarily to the cavils of unbelievers.*’

* Review, p. 19.

Here

Here is, firſt, a diſtinction which I confeſs I do not perfectly underſtand : To ſay,
the ſcriptures are not the word of God, but
only *contain* an account of it, ſeems to me
like ſaying, an act of Parliament is not the
law of the land, but only contains an account .
of the law of the land: for ſuch parts, at
leaſt, of the ſcripture as contain the chriſtian doctrine are certainly the word of God.
But the ſcriptures, we are told, never 'aſſume
' that title.' No! let us examine for ourſelves, for I much fear the Gentlemen that
ſay this are not, with all their criticiſm, well
acquainted with their Bible. I will cite
a few paſſages from both Teſtaments, and
let the candid reader compare the contexts.
When David, addreſſing Jehovah, ſays,
' *Thy word* is a lamp unto my feet, and a
' light unto my path † ;' did he not refer
to the ſacred writings of Moſes, which he
had in the preceeding verſes called, the *law*,
the precepts, the commandments, the teſti-
monies of Jehovah ?—' How ſweet are thy
' words unto my taſte !—Through thy pre-
' cepts I get underſtanding†.'

* Pſ. cxix. 105.
† Ibid, ver. 97 to 105. See the whole Pſalm.

In

In the New Teſtament, the ſcriptures are called ' the lively oracles,' and ' the oracles ' of God*;' expreſſions at leaſt equally ſtrong, and there are ſeveral paſſages where the very term ' Word of God' is not only moſt uſually, but moſt naturally underſtood as referring to them; though perhaps the expreſſion may ſtrictly intend, or at leaſt *include* the idea of divine Revelation, whether by the word preached or written.

What you ſay of the *plenary* inſpiration of the ſcriptures, might afford ſcope to a more extenſive enquiry than I can here inſtitute; but there is one queſtion which I beg leave to urge upon you with ſome ſeriouſneſs—Are the ſcriptures, particularly thoſe of the New Teſtament, to be conſidered as a *certain* and *infallible guide* to *divine truth*, or are they not? If they are—be ſo kind as to inform us what books and chapters are to be received as ſuch, and in what edition or tranſlation. For I have obſerved, that there is no one book or chapter but ſome or other Unitarian writer has rejected ; one admitting only the goſpel of Matthew,

---

* Acts vii. 38. Rom. iii. 2 Heb. v. 12. 1 Pet. iv. 11.

and

and another only that of Luke; and thofe
gentlemen who are liberal enough to admit
the four gofpels, generally deduct fuch chapters, and parts of chapters as are moft obnoxious to their fcheme. As to the Epiftolary parts, I believe you generally confider
them as the private opinions only of the
writers, and of little confequence to us: but
if fo, thofe writers muft have been guilty
of impofition ; particularly Peter, who claffes
the writings of his brother Paul among
the *other fcriptures**. On the other hand, if
the fcriptures do not contain any *certain* and
infallible guide to truth, it is of little confequence what they do contain: for if the
facred writers were the fubjects of Jewifh
or heathen prejudices, and if they were liable to errors and mifconceptions, your own
favourite ftudy of criticifm is indeed of little value; and it is of no more importance
to afcertain the true reading and accurate
Tranflation of Peter, John, or Paul, than
to fix the text and verfion of any of the
Greek or Latin Claffics. If we are only to
receive fuch parts of the Bible as *appear to*

* Eph. vi. 17. Heb. iv. 12. &c. &c.

us

us probable or juſt, then is this to make
'the word of God' of no effect.   To ſubmit
the divine oracles to the corrections of reaſon and philoſophy is an abſurdity equal to
any that can be found, even in the creed of
popery :—It is to exclude the ſunſhine, and
'rejoice in ſparks of our own kindling'—to
forſake the fountain of living waters, and to
hew out unto ourſelves broken ciſterns that
can hold no water.—A fault and a miſery,
Sir, from which I pray God to preſerve or
deliver you, and yours for the

'Truth's ſake, &c.

LETTER XV.

REV. SIR,

A Single Letter was much too short to consider your various objections under this head. I proceed therefore in the present Letter to observe,

5. Calvinists are represented as superstitious *Sabbatarians*—returning to Judaical customs, and running counter to the express injunctions of Paul—and to the very spirit of christianity, which, you tell us*, express- ' ly abolishes all distinction of days, and ' consequently the *Sabbath*.' On the contrary, it appears to me, that the Sabbath is not a Jewish institution, nor is it censured by the apostle.

That it was not merely a Jewish institution, appears from its appointment immediately on the creation. ' On the seventh day

---

* Review, p. 20.

' God

' God ended [or HAD ended *] his work
' which he had made : and he refted on the
' feventh day.' The Sabbath therefore was
a patriarchal inftitution, and in the book of
Genefis, there are fome pretty clear intimations of its obfervation by Abel, by Noah,
and by the other patriarchs, from whom it
doubtlefs fpread over moft ancient nations†.

We obferve a Sabbath therefore, not becaufe it was enjoined by Mofes, or obferved
by the Ifraelites; but becaufe it was a pre-
cept of the Creator from the beginning, and
never has been repealed, though the day itfelf has been changed, (and perhaps more
than once) as not belonging to the morality of the inftitution. I know that it has
been pretended, that Mofes mentions the Sabbath in this place by way of anticipation,
and that it was not obferved by the patriarchs.

---

* So the beft tranflators render it; but the Sama-
ritan (probably to avoid the apparent abfurdity of God
finifhing his work on the feventh day) reads, ' On
' the fixth day God ended his work, and he refted on
' the feventh.'

† See Kennicott's fecond Differtation, p. 180.—
Parkhurft's Lex. in שבע. Doddridge's Lect. prop. cxl.

This

This, however, I confider as an arbitrary
unfounded fuppofition; becaufe, it is certain
that the Ifraelites obferved a Sabbath before
the giving of the law at Sinai, for on occafion of the manna being rained from heaven,
on the fixth day of the week, Mofes thus
addreffed them, ' To-morrow is the reft of
' the holy Sabbath unto the Lord *.'

But this queftion may be drawn into a
narrower compafs, and fairly be decided
by your own fuffrage. ' Of public worfhip
' (you fay) I am a fincere advocate; and it
' having been the uniform practice of the
' chriftian church to affemble for this pur-
' pofe on the firft day of the week, I *highly*
' *approve* of the continuance of this *laudable*
' and *ufeful* cuftom. But that under the
' chriftian difpenfation one day is more holy
' than another, or that any employment or
' amufement, which is lawful on other days,
' is unlawful on the Sunday, can never be
' proved either from the fcriptures, or from
' ecclefiaftical antiquity †.' As you admit
the early affembly of chriftians on the firft
day of the week, which it fhould feem, was

---

* Exod. xvi. 23. &c.   † Review, p. 139.

B b   called

called the *Lord*'s-day*, as peculiarly devoted
to his fervice; permit me to appeal to you,
whether Confiſtency and Common-ſenſe
do not require, that a day appointed for
public worſhip ſhould be preſerved from ſecular buſineſs and amuſement? Or whether
any valuable purpoſe is likely to be anſwered
by the religious inſtructions mingled with
our public worſhip, if the buſy return immediately to their ſhops, and the gay and
idle to their diverſions?—You, Sir, are an
advocate for the Theatre (with what ſuccefs
we ſhall enquire preſently), but will you
plead for the decency, propriety, or conſiſtency, of adjourning thither from the houſe
of God? Or would you have our Sundays
cloſe, as did the laſt Thankſgiving day †—
(ſurely to the ſcandal of a chriſtian country)
—with the Lyar and the Beggar's Opera?

Infinite wiſdom has however decided this
point, by ordaining, in the firſt inſtance, the
Sabbath as a day of reſt; well knowing the
importance of ſecluding from ſecular con-
cerns the ſeaſon devoted to religious worſhip

* Rev. i. 10.
† Nov. 29, 1798. At Drury-lane Theatre.

and

and improvement: at the fame time, allowance is made for works of abfolute neceffity, and the utmoft latitude given for acts of benevolence and charity.

As to the authority of Paul, permit me to obferve, you have quoted him in exactly the manner for which you have cenfured Mr. Wilberforce and others; by exhibiting only detached paffages, without examining their tendency or dependence, from an inveftigation of which, it appears to me, that the apoftle had no reference to the queftion of obferving the Chriftian Sabbath; for, in both the epiftles you refer to, he is evidently fpeaking of inftitutions properly Jewifh. To the Coloffians*, he fays, 'Let no man judge ' you in meats or in drinks, or in refpect of ' a holy-day, or of the new moon, or of the ' Sabbath-days,' or rather Sabbaths, (for the word *days* is fupplementary), all which he declares were typical inftitutions, and therefore ceafed at Chrift's coming, to be obligatory. So in the paffage of Romans †, the obferving days is ranked with the obferving of meats; both therefore are equally parts of

* Chap. ii. 16.   † Chap. xiv,

                                    the

the Mofaic ritual; whereas, the Chriftian Sabbath ftands upon higher ground, and claims obfervance as a law given to our firft parent, and in him, to all mankind. It is true, that it was afterwards incorporated in the Jewifh code; but there, it occupies the fame refpectable place as the other precepts confeffedly moral, and the obfervation of the Sabbath is ranked with abftaining from idolatry and profanenefs. And this may account for the New Teftament not being more particular and exprefs upon the fubject. The keeping of *a* fabbath was not a fubject of difpute; nor could it be confiftently, where public worfhip was enjoined. If there were any difpute upon the fubject, I fhould fuppofe it muft relate to the particular day to be obferved, which being of little confequence, this 'authorifed Teacher ' permits every man to enjoy his own fenti- ' ments.'

But, before we difmifs this fubject, permit me to remonftrate a little with you on the tendency of this fentiment, as it refpects the prefent condition of mankind. There are many who will thank you for your notions of morality, in permitting them to go

from

from places of worſhip to places of diverſion, without impeachment of their chriſtianity; and numbers will admire your plan of mixing diverſions with religion; but are you aware what an injury you are offering to the lower claſſes of mankind? How often has the labourer hailed with bleſſings the return of this day!—a day which takes the yoke from off his ſhoulders, and gives a refpite to thoſe exertions which, if not intermitted, would foon exceed his ſtrength and overwhelm his ſpirits: a day which allows him to attend the worſhip of the Supreme, and implore a bleſſing on the labour of the other ſix: a day which permits him to enjoy, and to inſtruct his family: and which, in fine, enables him with new vigour, and recruited ſpirits, to recommence the buſineſs of the ſucceeding week.

But you will reply, perhaps the bulk of mankind do not thus enjoy this day. The more is it to be lamented if they abuſe the privilege, and that you ſhould encourage them ſo to do! But what would be the conſequence if all men thought with you? The avaricious maſter would demand the labour of his ſervants without intermiſſion; and

deprive

deprive them not only of the opportunities of ferving God, but of enjoying the chief comforts of private and of focial life. The apprentice and the menial fervant would be the flave of the covetuous and hard-hearted; and many individuals would facrifice their own health and even life, to the inordinate defire of amaffing wealth; for you, Sir, are too well acquainted with human nature not to know, that if no Sabbath was enjoined, none could be obferved, but by a few confcientious individuals to their own manifeft difadvantage, as is now the cafe in France.

As to the particular degree of ftrictnefs upon this day which fome perfons have enjoined, it is poffible it may have been carried to excefs. Piety may degenerate to fuperftition, and devotion to idolatry: but muft therefore piety and devotion be excluded from chriftianity? All extremes are to be avoided, but the danger of the prefent times is not of too much religion, but of too little: —not of keeping the Sabbath too ftrict, but of rejecting it altogether. Mr. Wilberforce is therefore to be juftified in reprefenting the indifference and contempt of profeffing chriftians in general, and efpecially among

among the higher claffes, as a proof of the low ftate of religion at prefent in this country.

6. A farther objection is taken againft the rigid morality of Mr. Wilberforce, and the Calvinifts, from their rejection and cenfure of *theatrical amufements*. ‘ No amufement,’ you think, ‘ is more innocent, or more rati- ‘ onal than that of a well-regulated theatre.’ It is ufelefs to talk of what exifts not. The queftion is not whether theatrical amufe- ments *might not* poffibly be conftructed on an unexceptionable plan ; but whether fuch amufements actually do exift ? and confider- ing the prefent ftate of mankind, whether it be not morally impoffible that they fhould ? I am not about to pollute thefe pages with ex- tracts from our theatrical writers. It is enough to afk one queftion ;—Suppofe a feries of dialogues to be written on the plan of our modern plays—fuppofe thefe dialogues to exhibit fcenes of villainy and debauchery —fuppofe the converfation of the different fpeakers to be interlarded, one with profane- nefs, and another with double entendre— Would you, Sir, recommend thefe as afford- ing innocent amufement? or would you
think

think them calculated to improve the morals
of our youth?

I even believe it impoffible to reform the
theatre without taking away every thing
which now interefts the generality of fpec-
tators, who are always beft entertained with
the exhibition of excentric, profane, and
even bafe characters. Farther, the performance itfelf muft have a bad effect upon the
morals of the actors as well as upon the au-
dience. From the performance of vicious
characters at the playhoufe to that of bafe
and immortal actions in real life, is an eafy,
dangerous tranfition: and thofe accuftomed
to applaud the former, will hardly be taught
thereby, to avoid and to abhor the latter.
This appears to me an objection which cannot be obviated, without the public tafte
could be directed to the love of virtue only,
and be taught to abhor vice in all its ap-
pearances, fictitious as well as real.

It has been often faid that theatres tend to
reform the morals of a people, but an inftance
of that nature has never, to my knowledge,
been produced: while of the contrary effect
the examples are many and notorious. But
inftead of grave argument I will quote
autho-

authority—an authority the moſt unexceptionable. The late celebrated and facetious
Ned Shuter, (as he was familiarly called) it
is well known was, at times, under ſerious
impreſſions, and occaſionally a hearer of Mr.
Whitefield and Mr. Kinſman. Meeting with
the latter once at Plymouth, after the lives
both of Mr. K. and himſelf had been en-
dangered by exertions in their reſpective pro-
feſſions, Mr. S. thus addreſſed him. ‘ Had
‘ you died, it would have been in ſerving
‘ the beſt of maſters ; but had I, it would
‘ have been in the ſervice of the devil.’ In
farther converſation, Mr. S. added—‘ My
‘ Lord E. ſent for me to-day, and I was glad
‘ I could not go.—Poor things ! they are
‘ unhappy, and they want Shuter to make
‘ them laugh. But, O Sir !—ſuch a life as
‘ yours ! As ſoon as I leave you I ſhall be
‘ King Richard. This is what they call a
‘ good play ; as good as ſome ſermons. I
‘ acknowledge there are ſome ſtriking and
‘ moral things in it. But after it, I ſhall
‘ come in again with my farce of *A diſh of
‘ all ſorts,* and knock all that on the head.
‘ Fine reformers are we *!’—Such is the

* Evangelical Mag. vol. i. p. 52.

C c   character

character of the theatre even from a per-
former.

Once more under this article, permit me
to transcribe a passage from your own work
in speaking of the Sabbath. ' The christian
' law,' you say, ' expressly requires, not
' that a seventh part only, but that the whole
' of our time, and every action of life, should
' be devoted to the service of God ; and that
" whether we eat or drink, or whatever
" we do, we should do all to his glory." So
' that to a true christian every day is a Sab-
' bath ; and every employment is an act of
' devotion *.'—So then, Sir, we must attend
the theatre for the glory of God—perform
our devotions at a farce, and call this rational
religion ! ! !

But the most ' gross and pernicious error'
charged upon us is, that of ' *christian idola-*
' *try*, or the worship of the Son and Spirit,
' together with the Father ;' a crime which,
though not of equal magnitude with *heathen*
idolatry, as ' not productive of similar im-
' moralities,' is yet ' much to be censured
' and lamented, and carefully to be avoid-
' ed †.'

* Review, p. 140.   † Ibid. p. 129.

You

You admit, indeed, a degree of ' rational
' regard' may be due to Jefus, and is by
' himfelf required :'—you ' revere his me-
' mory as the moft excellent of human char-
' acters, and the moft eminent of all the pro-
' phets :'—you profefs joyfully to ' embrace
'. his doctrine, confide in his promife, and
' bow to his authority.' Yet you are confident that there ' can be no proper founda-
' tion for religious *addreffes* to him, nor of
' *gratitude* for favours now received, nor yet
' of *confidence* in his future interpofition in
' our behalf. All affections and addreffes of
' this nature,' you therefore ' confider as un-
' authorized by the chriftian revelation, and
' infringements on the prerogative of God *.'

It would not be eafy, perhaps, to find any
where a more pointed contradiction than this
paffage affords to the affertions of the New
Teftament writers, in three important particulars. (1.) You fay, there can be ' no foun-
' dation for religious *addreffes*' to Chrift;
Paul fays, he *befought* the Lord thrice, evidently referring to Chrift, in whofe ftrength
he triumphed †. (2.) You add, ' nor of *grati-*

---

* Review, p. 84, 85.   † 1 Cor. xii. 8, 9.

tude

' *tude* for favours now received.' Paul faid,
' I *thank* Chrift Jefus our Lord, who hath
' enabled me, for that he counted me faithful,
' putting me into the miniftry*.' (3.) ' Nor
' of confidence in his future interpofitions :'
the author of the epiftle to the Hebrews fays,
' Jefus is able to fave to the uttermoft all
' that come unto God by him, feeing he
' ever liveth to make *interceffion* for them.†'
Such is the harmony between the fcriptures
and your enlightned and philofophic fyftem:
and fuch is the refined love you profefs to
the Saviour ; a love divefted both of *grati-*
tude and *confidence,* and which forbids all
communion with him !

But the Chrift we worfhip you confider as
a creature of our own imagination, as ' fuch
' a being as' has ' in fact no real exiftence ;'
confequently, all the affections founded on
thefe ideas, as ' vain and illufory, varying ac-
' cording to the variable fancies of men, and
' incapable of conftituting wife and perma-
' nent principles of action ‡.' The *wifdom*
of this principle muft certainly be referred to
the better judgment of rational critics, and

---

* 1 Tim. i. 12. † Heb.vii. 25. ‡ Review. 86.

men

men of philofophic minds; but that the principle is capable of real, great, and permanent *effects*, it is fufficient that I appeal to that ' noble army of martyrs and confeffors,' who, actuated thereby, have forfaken all things, not counting their own lives dear unto them for the fake of this ' ideal, this ' imaginary Chrift.' If you, Sir, will condefcend to inform us, what fuperior effects have refulted from your view of the fubject, then fhall we be able to judge how far this miftaken devotion falls fhort of ' that digni-' fied and manly piety, which is the natural ' refult of proper attention to' your ' more ' juft and rational principles.' Until then, however, we muft be permitted ftill to act upon a principle that has been the common ftimulus of apoftles, faints, and martyrs.

Having thus, Sir, gone through the various charges you have exhibited againft the popular, orthodox, or Calviniftic writers, as you indifferently call them—let me conclude with a recapitulation of your charges againft them, or rather againft *us*—for I confefs myfelf ambitious for a fhare in the honours of your cenfure, and the glorious ftigma of the crofs.

Firft,

First, it seems we have too mean, humble
and unworthy thoughts of ourselves. Instead
of boasting that we are as our Creator made
us*—we confess that we are sinners of great
magnitude, and abhor ourselves in dust and
ashes. Instead of trusting in ourselves that
we are righteous, we account ' all things
' but loss for Christ's sake, that we may
' be found in him, not having our own
' righteousness which is of the law, but that
' which is through the faith of Christ, the
' righteousness which is of God by faith.'
Instead of mixing in the fashionable di-,
versions of the age, and conforming our
tempers and manners to the world—Instead
of accounting all days alike, and mingling
business, amusements, and devotion—we
study non-conformity to the world; are
fearful of listening to its maxims, and drinking in its spirit; and are, in short, so Jewish
and antiquated in our notions, that we do
not frequent the theatres, and we keep holy
the sabbath-day.

Instead of arraigning the goodness, and
even justice of our Maker, because his ways

* Review, p 56, 57.

are

are often infcrutible to our weak underftand-
ings, we lie proftrate in the duft, and confefs that ' fhame and confufion of face be-
' longeth unto us, and mercy and forgive-
' nefs unto the Lord our God.'

Inftead of confidering the Lord our Saviour as altogether fuch an one as ourfelves,
and regarding him with the cold philofophical efteem of rational chriftians, we love, we
reverence, we adore him. We honour the
Son, even as we honour the Father; and with
the whole company of faints and angels,
afcribe ' Bleffing and honour and glory and
' power, unto him that fitteth upon the throne,
' and unto the Lamb for ever and ever.'

Thefe, Sir, are, as Calvinifts, our follies,
and our crimes; and having nothing better
to offer in our defence, than you have already feen, I leave them with all their force
upon the minds of our Readers.—As to you,
Sir, permit me to form one wifh—that in a
dying hour you may enjoy all the confidence,
and comfort which thefe fentiments, and a
correfpondent conduct have infpired in the
breafts of believers, in all ages and in all countries.

I remain finally yours, &c.

T. W.

APPENDIX.

ADDRESSED TO THE AUTHOR OF

LETTERS ON

HEREDITARY DEPRAVITY.

LETTER XVI.

Additional Remarks on the Authority of Scripture in this Controversy.

SIR,

JUST as the above MS. was prepared for prefs, I faw your Letters advertifed to *bind up* with Mr. Belfham's, and it immediately occured to me, as proper to examine them, before I obtruded my obfervations on the public ; fince it might prove that you had elucidated fome of his paradoxes, or obviated fome of his miftakes. And though, in this refpect I am difappointed, I confefs myfelf perfectly fatisfied that, whatever becomes of your caufe, your friends have rea-

fon

fon to congratulate themfelves, that it is in no danger of fuffering from the want of zeal or talents, while it is in the hands of fuch able advocates as yourfelf and Mr. B.; efpecially in contending with Calvinifts, who, as you very modeftly infinuate, muft, to be fure, be too much depraved in intellect to contend with Unitarians, or even to merit their attention *. Under all thefe difadvantages, however, we are not dejected nor difcouraged: we neither afk for quarter, nor retreat. We know that *great is the truth, and muft ultimately prevail;* and therefore, if you would have the *courtefy* to permit a brother Layman to whifper in your ear, he would fuggeft the falutary hint of Ahab to Benhadad—' Let not him that putteth on ' his armour boaft himfelf as he that putteth ' it off †.'

Were victory my object, and were it to depend upon a difplay of fuperior ability, I could have no hope in contending with a philofopher of your fize. Should I, however, be defeated and put to filence, I fhould not have the mortification to reflect that it were

* Letters on Hereditary Depravity, p. 169.

† 1 Kings, xx. 11.

D d

by

by a writer of defective intellect. No, Sir, the difeafe of human nature is feated rather in the heart than in the head: and the judgment is depraved, not by a derangement of the faculties, as you infinuate we maintain*, but by the afcendency of carnal appetites and corrupt affections.

But truth, and not victory, is the object of thefe Letters. Were I convinced that the principles here defended are not the doctrines of the Bible, or that they tend to fully the glory of the divine perfections, I hope I fhould poffefs honefty and honour enough to pronounce thofe hard words—*I was miftaken.* This at prefent, indeed, appears impoffible; and while my views remain the fame, and feeling the great comfort and importance of the Calviniftic doctrines, may I not be permitted to be their humble apologift, and plead even with you, Sir, who, by the fuperior lights of reafon and philofophy, have been tempted to renounce them?

So far as you tread in the fteps of Mr B. it cannot be neceffary for me to trace you. Where your arguments or objections are the

* Letters, p. 169.

fame

fame, the fame anfwers may apply. But when you tread new ground, and advance new arguments either from fcripture or from reafon, I fhall venture to follow you with animadverfions and remarks. The prefent Letter will be confined to what you fay on the *authority* of fcripture, and its *evidence* on the fubject of human, or (as you term it) *Hereditary Depravity*.

On the authority of fcripture as a teft of truth, I have already addreffed a Letter to Mr. B. ; but as this is the hinge on which the controverfy chiefly turns, I fhall take the liberty of fubjoining a farther remark on this fubject.

I obferve, that both you and Mr. B. refpect the fcriptures fo far as you think they countenance your opinions; but wherever they appear adverfe, you reduce their authority to a mere nullity.

Chriftians of your defcription indeed acknowledge, that the *word of God* ought to be implicitly received; but then you admit nothing to be the word of God but what agrees perfectly with your pre-conceived opinions. It is in vain to plead the authority of prophets or apoftles, or of Jefus Chrift himfelf;

D d 2 fince

fince with you, *reafon*, and reafon *alone* muft
be the guide. ' When a doctrine is pro-
' pofed which evidently contradicts' in *your*
view of it, ' firft principles univerfally ad-
' mitted', you ' reject it*,' without enquiring
from what authority it comes.—Here, Sir,
permit me to fay, language of this kind would
not be tolerated in a Calvinift. Suppofing the
doctrines of Calvinifm to contradict ' firft
' principles univerfally admitted', which is
the point you fhould have proved; you fuper-
cede all evidence from revelation, by direct-
ing. your enquiries, not into the validity of
fcripture proofs, but fimply into the agree-
ment of the propofed doctrine with your
firft principles previoufly affumed.

But let us hear your argument; you think
' It is infinitely more natural to fufpect that
' a wrong interpretation is given by weak
' and fallible men, to thofe fcriptural ex-
' preffions which are thought to contain the
' fentiment enforced, than that it fhould be
' in reality the word of God. Since fcrip-
' ture phrafeology is fo *extremely various,*
' that every rafh and inconfiderate mortal

* Letters, page 35, 36.

' may

' may find out fome expreffions that fhall
' feem to countenance his favourite dog-
' mata:' you therefore ' think it highly ne-
' ceffary to lay down for' yourfelves, ' fome
' indubitable pofitions, which may fafely
' conduct' you ' through the labyrinths of
' error and contrarieties *.'

As you have done as the honour to compare the doctrines of Calvinifm with thofe
of Popery, and even with its moft abfurd
tenet, Tranfubftantiation † ; you cannot
juftly be offended, if I return the compliment, by obferving the perfect correfpond-
ence between your argument in favour of
reafon, with that of the Catholics in favour
of the authority of the church. They fpeak
with the fame contempt as you do of the
facred writings, and the danger of miftak-
ing fcriptural expreffions; only, inftead of recurring to your ' firft principles,' they appeal to a *living head*, and certainly have the
advantage in this refpect. However, the parallel may fhew, as was my defign in ftating
it, that Popery and Unitarianifm are alike
enemies to the Bible; and treat it as the Sa-

* P. 36.   † P. 23.

viour

viour of mankind was treated upon Calvary, when he was on both hands derided and blafphemed. For if fcripture has no authority further than it agrees with your ' firft ' principles,' or their *ci-devant* Oracle at Rome—If either reafon or tradition is *alone* to be ' the guide,' of what ufe, give me leave to afk, is fcripture ? Might we not do juft as well without it, and fave infinite perplexity thereby ?

But, in juftice to your argument, let us attend to its application, and confider the particular inftance in which you try a propofed doctrine by your ' firft principles uni-- ' verfally admitted.' You ' know, for ex- ' ample, that the *God of grace* cannot poffefs ' a character effentially different from the ' *God of nature*, fince he is the fame God :' You ' *naturally expect* much clearer difplays ' of univerfal benignity under the former ' character, than thofe which the latter ex- ' hibits to' your ' admiring view; and ' therefore *fufpect* thofe doctrines which ' create an oppofition *.' Now this fuppofes, in the firft place, that the character

* Letters, p; 36.

of

of ' the God of nature' is certainly more obvious and determinate than the character of
the ' God of grace,' fince you make the
former a criterion of the latter ; but this is
not a ' principle univerfally admitted,' and
therefore not one of thofe on which you
profefs to argue. You know, Sir, we take
the oppofite courfe to harmonize thefe fubjects ; and believing the light of Revelation
to be fuperior to that of Nature, explain
the character of the God of nature in conformity to that of the God of grace.

Again, you ' *naturally expect* much clearer
' difplays of univerfal benignity under the
' character of the God of grace', than are
exhibited in the other character. Probably
you may ; but do you mean to fet down *your
natural expectations* for ' firft principles uni-
' verfally admitted ?' If not, they are nothing
to our purpofe. I do not mean, however, to
difpute the fact. I conceive even the Calviniftic doctrines, horrid as they feem to you,
reprefent the God of grace as infinitely more
benignant than the God of nature appears,
either in creation, or in your liberal notions of
his character ; and no lefs *univerfally* fo, fince
nature does not, any more than fcripture, re-
pre-

prefent God as indifferent to moral evil, or benignant to finners obftinately and finally impenitent. We deny, therefore, that our doctrines create an oppofition, or give any juft
reafon for fuch fufpicions. Upon the whole
then, your demonftration, founded on firft
principles, dwindles into a *fufpicion* founded
upon a miftake arifing from your own prejudices and mifconceptions.

But principles, as well as perfons, when
they become fufpected, muft hope for no
very lenient treatment : it is well, however,
if they may be brought to trial ; and we
have no objection that *fair criticifm*, if it
may deferve that name, fhould be the judge.
It might feem reafonable, that the fcriptures fhould be heard in their own defence.
But this is too much to be expected : if admitted at all, it muft be in fuch parts only as
favour, or may be fuppofed to favour, the
caufe of our opponents. For thefe ' diftin-
' guifh *moft* carefully, the plain and fimple
' truths exprefsly taught by Chrift himfelf
' and his apoftles, *after* they were commif-
' fioned by their Mafter to preach the gofpel,
' from thofe ftrong figurative expreffions,
' and bold reprefentations, occafionally employed

' ployed by the fame apoftles in their epifto-
' lary writings; where, it is the invariable
' object, not to preach *another* gofpel, nor
' make an *addition* to that preached in their
' perfonal miniftry ; but to inforce the truths
' already promulgated, upon the hearts and
' confciences of the new converts to chrif-
' tianity * .'

Does not this paffage, in the firft place,
imply that the epiftolary writings of the New
Teftament were written *before* the apoftles
were commiffioned to preach? If fo, it would
fufficiently account for their being lefs correct and explicit in their doctrine ; but, as
you know the direct contrary to be the fact,
it naturally leans in our favour; for it is not
ufual for men to leffen in judgment as they
encreafe in wifdom and experience.

But their object, you fay, was not to
preach ' another gofpel.' True, and for this
reafon, we conclude they taught the fame
doctrines in their fermons as in their Letters,
only, we have the latter at length, and the
former in abridgment. To which may be
added, that the former being addreffed ge-

* Review, p. 37, 38.

E e

nerally

nerally to a mixed multitude, were in great
meafure confined to firſt principles, whereas
the epiſtles were directed to believers, ‘ going
‘ on unto perfection,’ and confequently, went
farther into the peculiar tenets of chriſtianity.

You admit, that ‘ the abettors of the Cal-
‘ viniſtic doctrines act confiſtently, in being
‘ ſtrenuous for the ſupport of original de-
‘ pravity ; for they juſtly view it as the _foun-_
‘ _dation_ of a fyſtem which they have miſ-
‘ taken for genuine chriſtianity, and which
‘ cannot be ſubverted without the demoliti-
‘ on of the ſuperſtructure*.’ This doctrine is indeed a fundamental principle ; but
when you infinuate that we difplace Jeſus
Chriſt the true foundation, in order to lay
that of Hereditary Depravity†, I cannot
acquit you of difingenuity and grofs mifreprefentation, in taking the advantage of a
common ambiguity of language. Human
depravity is certainly a fundamental principle in chriſtianity, and the knowledge of
this may be confidered as a foundation of our
theology, ‘in the fame fenfe as a knowledge

* Letters, p. 42.   † Ibid, p. 38.

of

of difeafes may be confidered as the foundation of medical fcience: but does this prevent the knowledge of medicine from being equally fundamental ? Chrift is indeed the foundation of our faith, our hope, and our obedience; but how you, who reject his Deity, atonement, and interceffion, can pretend that ' faith in Chrift is the foundation' of your fcheme, I confefs I know not. You feem to admit him to have been a good man, a moral philofopher and a prophet; but if he were no more, I fee not why any other philofopher might not do as well—perhaps better; for I recollect, that Dr. Prieftley, though he admits that Jefus taught the truth in a popular way, yet very much doubts whether, in fome inftances, he accurately and properly underftood it ! ! !* But I turn from fuch impieties with difguft, to adore the injured Saviour, and to recommend to his compaffionate regard, thofe that revile and perfecute him, not knowing what they do. That this mercy may extend to you, Sir, is the fincere and fervent wifh of,

You ready fervant in the caufe of Truth.

T. W.

* Prieftley on Neceffity, § xi.

LETTER XVII.

Of Man's Original State and Fall.

Sir,

AS it is not my object to defend any human scheme, or systematic definitions of this doctrine, I pass over your long extracts from protestant catechisms and confessions. I wish to keep as near as possible to the simplicity of the inspired writers, and plead for their literal and obvious sense, in opposition to those who would reduce all the doctrines of the Bible to figurative and poetic forms of speech. If, on the other hand, some good men have carried their creeds and confessions beyond the scriptures, I do not consider myself bound to follow them: the closer we keep to the language and doctrine of inspiration, the better.

It appears evident to me, that the sacred writers speak of man under the different states of innocent and fallen, which you, and other Unitarian writers, confound together. In the first instance, they describe the whole

whole creation as *very good*, and man in particular as created in the *image of God* *. This
expreſſion you refer to *dominion* only, whereas
the apoſtle expreſsly refers it to *knowledge*
alſo; and in another place to *righteouſneſs*
and *true holineſs*. 'The new man, renew-
'ed in knowledge, after him that created
'him.'—'The new man after God [i. e.
'after the image of God] is renewed in righ-
'teouſneſs and true holineſs.†'

To make the image of God conſiſt only
in dominion, is to repreſent the Deity rather
as an arbitary tyrant than as a being of infinite perfections. Mr. Bulkeley more judi-
ciouſly includes the reſemblance of his intelligence, and moral excellence, as well as
government ‡.

'God made man [men or mankind] up-
'right; but they have ſought out many in-
'ventions‖,' or devices: an expreſſion which
does not indeed refer ſimply and 'excluſive-
ly to that act of our firſt parents, which
'brought death into the world, and all
'our woe;' but includes the various wicked

* Gen. i. 27, 31.   † Col. iii. 10.   Eph. iv. 24.
‡ Apology, p. 21, &c.   ‖ Eccles. vii. 29.

devices of their pofterity, by which the depravity originating in their defection, has encreafed in its propagation; ftill, however, it afferts the fact for which it was produced, that man is fallen, degenerated and depraved.

It has been common to argue this point alfo from the introduction of mortality, efpecially the mortality of children. So Paul himfelf; ' Wherefore, as by one man fin ' entered into the world, and death by fin, fo ' death paffed upon all men, for that all have ' finned. For, until the law fin was in the ' world: but fin is not imputed where there ' is no law. Neverthelefs death reigned from ' Adam to Mofes, even over them that had ' not finned, after the fimilitude of Adam's ' tranfgreffion'—namely, infants, who were not yet chargeable with actual iniquity. He therefore concludes in the fubfequent verfes, that ' by one man's difobedience many ' were made finners;' and that ' by the offence ' of one, judgment came upon all men unto ' condemnation.'—That fin reigned unto ' death'—and in the next chapter, ' that the ' wages of fin is death.*'

Moft

Moſt of the above facts and aſſertions you have controverted—' God made man upright ' —in his own image—very good,' ſay the ſcriptures. ' We may innocently preſume,' ſay you, ' that the powers and faculties of ' Adam and Eve were as limited as our own, ' and that their *propenſities* to good and *evil* ' were *perfectly ſimilar**' to ours. Either then *we* have no propenſities to evil, or *they* had the ſame. The latter I preſume is not your ſentiment, and the former has been ſhewn irreconcileable either to ſcripture or to fact†.

' In the infantile ſtate of the world,' you think, ' it was the eaſieſt thing in nature to ' be innocent, for ſcarcely could a vice be ' committed‡.' If ſo, how aggravated was their crime to ſin, when obedience was ſo eaſy, and vice ſo difficult! and yet, with a ſtrange inconſiſtency, you attempt to prove their crime was too inconſiderable to merit any thing farther than temporal death ; and that, even this was not ſo much introduced as a puniſhment, as a convenience and a bleſſing.

* Letters, p. 60.　† See above, Letters iii. iv. and v.
‡ Letters, p. 61.

Your

Your words are, ' Let us remember, that
' as life is the free gift of God, the conti-
' nuation of our exiſtence to a *perpetuity*
' cannot be claimed by us as a natural right.
' We may add, that it would prove a *perpe-*
' *tual curſe* before the minds of men were
' fully prepared for ſo vaſt a deſign.*'—Yes!
' Perpetuity of life,' or immortality, in paradiſe ' a perpetual curſe!!' Surely, Sir, whatever your averſion may be to myſteries,
you muſt have a peculiar delight in paradoxes, to repreſent immortality, the firſt
great bleſſing of the goſpel, as a perpetual
curſe to men in their moſt innocent and
happy ſtate!—But, perhaps the laſt clauſe
was meant to ſave your conſiſtency—' before
' the minds of men were prepared for ſo vaſt
' a deſign!' So then, men are not prepared
for immortality by innocence and happineſs,
as in the golden age of primeval exiſtence ;
but after they were depraved and wretched!
—This, I ſuppoſe, is one of the lucid principles of rational divinity.

It is granted, that ' infinite wiſdom is able
' to convert the greateſt ſeeming evil into

* Letters, p. 63.

' the

‘ the moſt ſubſtantial good,’ and to the true
chriſtian, even death itſelf is made a bleſſing;
but why you ſhould here introduce an en-
comium on death; and a cenſure on immortality, I am at a loſs to conceive; unleſs it
be to offer an apology for ſin—to repreſent
it as a trifle that could not provoke the Deity
to any ſevere reſentment, nor bring down
any real puniſhment; but only a temporary
inconvenience, that in the end muſt be a
great advantage.

But you have elſewhere admitted, that
death was threatned as the penalty of tranſ-
greſſion—that it was an object of terror to our
firſt parents—and afterward denounced as its
juſt and final puniſhment *. Now, Sir,
would you be underſtood to mean, that the
Deity made ‘ a moſt ſubſtantial good’ the
penalty of ſin? Surely, if immortality were
in itſelf ‘ a perpetual curſe,’ that ſhould have
been the puniſhment of ſin; and death, as
a ‘ moſt ſubſtantial good,’ the reward of
obedience and fidelity.

But the reference juſt made, leads me to
notice your decided opinion on the nature of

* See Letters p. 128, 129,

F f   the

the death threatened to our firſt progenitors,, which you are confident could extend no farther than the *literal* meaning of that ex-preſſion, ' Duſt thou art, and unto duſt ſhalt ' thou return.' Permit me, in this place, to aſk a few queſtions. Do you believe a ſtate of future puniſhment? Is not that puniſh-ment a ſecond death? Was it not threatened under the idea of death? Why might it not then be included in the firſt threatening—in the firſt ſentence? Indeed the contrary ſup-poſition is attended with difficulties that I am perſuaded you have not conſidered. You, doubtleſs, admit the doctrine of a future life, and that Adam, as well as his poſterity, were ſubjects of it, conſequently, expoſed to its penalties, as well as intitled to its rewards. Do you then ſuppoſe that God would inflict ſuch a puniſhment without warning ſinners of it? Or if he did threaten it, under what term is it expreſſed beſide that of death?

To ſay, this is recurring to a figurative ſenſe, is no objection, ſince in the firſt ſtage of language it is highly figurative. Many Unitarian writers reduce the whole hiſtory of the fall to allegory, though I think un-juſtly. Why then object to the figurative

ufe

ufe of a term fo frequently ufed figuratively
in fcripture ? Might I not add the ftyle of
Mofes, and the very genius of the. language
evidently require it ? The trees of knowledge and of life—the feed of the ferpent and
of the woman—are evidently metaphorical ;
and even the term *life* frequently includes
happinefs : Why then may not the term
death include mifery and pain ?

Do you ftill afk, what concern have we in
this tranfaction of our firft parent ? Or what
part have we either in his crime or punifhment ? The anfwer to this depends on another queftion—Was Adam a diftinct ifolated
individual like each of us ? Or was he the
federal head of his pofterity ? The former
appears to be your hypothefis, and the latter
mine.

If we recur to the original hiftory, it is
true that Adam is fpoken of throughout as an
individual, with little or no *exprefs* reference
to his offspring ; but are they not, therefore,
to be underftood as equally interefted in the
prohibition and the threatning ? Was our
firft parent to be expofed to death alone, and
his pofterity to be immortal ? Was Eve only
to conceive in forrow ? Or Adam alone to

F f 2 fweat

fweat, and labour, and return to duft? You will not fuppofe this, becaufe you tell us, on the authority of an apoftle, that ' in ' Adam all die.'—Suppofe, on the other hand, our firft parents had preferved their innocence, were they to live in paradife alone? were not their pofterity alfo to be happy and immortal? But if mankind at large would have reaped bleffings from their obedience—if they have fuffered the multiform curfe of labour, ficknefs, and death from their difobedience, do not thefe circumftances prove that we are deeply interefted in the conduct and fate of Adam, and is not this tantamount to what Calviniftic divines intend by the covenant between God and him?

But if we are involved in the punifhment of Adam's fin, we are involved in the whole of it, for there feems no poffible way of our being involved only in a part. If we are expofed to death thereby, we are expofed to all the evils included in that term, and confequently to future punifhment—unlefs you will pretend that the punifhment of fin extends no farther than the prefent life. And if the punifhment of fin be eternal, then are

we

we expofed unto eternal punifhment. But on this queftion I have made fome remarks in a preceding Letter *.

To return—Had we no facred book but that of Genefis, I think we muft admit that mankind are involved in the whole penalty of Adam's fin, or roundly deny their intereft in any part of it, and particularly in mortality; but as we have the New Teftament, if we admit the teftimony of Paul, the point is perfectly determinate and clear—obferving by the way, that the apoftle repeatedly compares Chrift and Adam as the heads and reprefentatives of their refpective offspring. All in Adam died in him—all in Chrift live in him. As by one man's offence many were made finners, fo by the obedience of one fhall many be made righteous. That the latter, Sir, may be your happinefs as well as mine, is the fincere wifh of

Your humble fervant, &c.

* Letter vii. near the clofe:

LETTER XVIII.

*Scripture Proofs of Natural Depravity vindi-
cated ; and its Confiftency with other Doctrines of Scripture.*

SIR,

HOWEVER rational and philofophical
may be the Unitarian fcheme, it muft,
I think, be obvious to every impartial obfer-
ver that it cannot derive much fupport from
the Bible ; and that the *forte* of its advocates
does not confift in fcripture evidence. Indeed the moft, in general, that thefe Gentlemen attempt is, to ward off the arrows
aimed againft them from that quarter ; and
even in this, I conceive their fuccefs is far
from being proportionate to their zeal. This
remark will, I apprehend, apply to your animadverfions, and Mr. Belfham's, on the
evidence produced by Mr. Wilberforce.
Part of your objections, as well as Mr. B.'s
have been already confidered, and there are
but two inftances, as I recollect, which appear to me to require farther obfervation.

The

The firſt, of theſe relates to an expreſſion of David, who acknowledges his being born in ſin. You coincide with Mr. Bulkley's idea*; and conceive, that ' He adopted a ' phraſe *proverbial* among the Jews, by which ' he intimated that his vicious propenſities ' were ſo great, that had he been born with ' them, they could not have been ſtronger. That this expreſſion was proverbial in the time of David you offer no proof within a thouſand years; and, judging from circum-ſtances, I ſhould be much more inclined to believe that the expreſſion became proverbial from David's uſe of it, than that he adopted it becauſe proverbial. The uſe, however, of a ſimilar expreſſion by two perſons, ſup-poſing them contemporary, will not prove it to be a proverb; nor will its being prover-bial prove it to have little or no meaning: indeed, the emphaſis you have yourſelf given to the words†, is ſufficient to overturn your own hypotheſis: for if David's propenſities to ſin could not have been ſtronger had he been born with them, you ſuppoſe him as much under the influence of theſe propen-

* See above, p. 21.   † Letters, p. 72.

ſities

fities, and as unable to refift them, as we poffibly can do.

As to the expreffion ' born in fins' ufed by the Pharifees, I doubt much if it had any allufion or relation to that of the pfalmift. The occafion of the words will give a better light into their meaning. The Pythagorean notion of the tranfmigration of fouls, it fhould feem obtained pretty early among the Jews. The author of the apocryphal book of Wifdom appears to allude to it, when he fays, ' being good, I entered into a body ' undefiled *;' implying both a previous ex- iftence, and that a refidence in blemifhed or defective bodies, was a kind of punifhment for the vices of a former ftate. Such ideas alfo the difciples of our Lord appear to have entertained, when they afked him, faying, ' Mafter, did this man fin, or his parents, ' that he was born blind † ?' affuming that fo grievous a calamity muft have been owing to fome remarkable caufe ; either as a judg- ment on his parents for a heinous crime, or a punifhment on himfelf for vices committed in a previous ftate. But the Pharifees, not

* Wifdom viii. 20.   † John ix. 2.

hefitating

hesitating like the disciples, boldly fix the cause upon the man himself—' Thou wast ' *altogether* born in sins, and dost thou teach ' us *?' As if they had said, ' Thou art an ' old offender—a sinner before thy. birth ' here, and suffering the punishment of thy ' sins.' It does not appear that these passages have any reference to original sin, consequently, they determine nothing respecting it ; but I confess, I cannot help considering these Pythagorean, or Platonic notions, as corruptions of the scripture doctrine of original sin, and an attempt to render it more rational and palatable to philosophic minds.

The other passage on which you have animadverted, has been also considered in my Letters to Mr. Belsham†. I have only farther to remark upon the terms, ' *by nature* ' children of wrath, &c.' that though I cannot here go through the several passages in which the expression is used in scripture, I am fully satisfied, from a careful examination, that it always intends something con-natural to us, either originally or adventitiously :

* John ix. 34.   † Eph. ii. 3.   See above, p. 29.

G g   and

and in the text, which looks moſt favourably
toward the ſenſe of *cuſtom*, I have the
authority of Le Clerc himſelf for ſaying,
that it ſignifies neither cuſtom nor diſpoſition; but is oppoſed to inſtruction *: i. e. it
ſignifies what is derived from *nature* previous
to inſtruction or example.

Having, as you ſuppoſe, warded off the
force of ſcripture evidence on this queſtion,
you endeavour, in a few inſtances, to ſhew,
that the doctrine for which we plead is abſolutely inconſiſtent with other doctrines admitted and owned by us, and eſpecially
with the following:

Firſt, You think it totally deſtroys ' all the
' ſubſequent *temptations* of Satan †.'—Juſt
the contrary; the depravity of the heart is
what the temptations of the enemy chiefly
act upon: it is the traitor within that opens
to him the citadel. Satan could not prevail
againſt Jeſus, becauſe he had nothing in
him ‡; he prevails againſt us becauſe he has
ſo much.

Again, Original Depravity oppoſes ' the
' true and proper *incarnation* of the Son of

* Le Clerc on Hammond, in 1 Cor. xi. 14.
† Letters, p. 117.   ‡ John xiv. 30.

' God.'

'God *.' How so? Human nature is depraved, and could not in the course of ordinary generation, or *without a miracle*, be propagated pure; and therefore—what? It could not be rendered pure by the *immediate* and *miraculous* agency of the Holy Spirit. Is not this answered in the very statement?—So much for this boasted argument that could not be evaded!

In other parts of your work, you represent the same doctrine as highly incompatible with the divine perfections, as revealed in scripture, and even understood by Calvinists themselves. Thus particularly, you insinuate the inconsistency of ' offers to penitent ' sinners of pardon, grace, and strength,' as but a mockery and an insult to the *non-elect*, who have no power to receive them; and the actual bestowment of these blessings on the elect as an injury and injustice to the world at large. Such is the tendency (as I suppose you will admit) of the reasoning in your first Letter †; and this has been more forcibly and explicitly urged by other writers on the same side, particularly Dr. Priestley ‡.

---

* Letters, p. 118.　† See page 16, 17, and note.
‡ On Necessity, § xii.

My

My limits will not admit of going at length into this inquiry; but I would beg leave to fuggeft an hint, which, whatever may be its effect on others, fhould filence gentlemen who adopt the fcheme of Philofophical Neceffity, as is now generally the cafe, I believe, with Unitarians.—For every thing that can be urged on this queftion may be reduced to this principle, that creatures of neceffity *cannot* be the fubjects of duties or motives—virtue or vice—praife or blame —reward or punifhment; whereas Dr. Prieftley himfelf has, I think, very fatisfactorily proved that it is upon this principle alone they *can* be either*. Now, if a divine predetermination of the prefent circumftances, and future fate of an individual do not prevent his being the proper fubject of duties and motives, of virtue and vice, &c. where is the inconfiftency of exhorting or enjoining upon him things, not naturally impoffible, but only accidentally or morally fo, by the pre-ordination and arrangement of circumftances? The Neceffarian, who believes the objects of future punifhment

* On Neceffity, § vii.

certain

certain and determined, admits the very thing which he charges as an inconfiftency upon the Calvinift: for whether future punifhment be temporary or final, vindictive or corrective, will make no difference on this queftion. ' It is only (as Dr. P. farther ' obferves) where the neceffity of finning ' arifes from fome other caufe than a man's ' own *difpofition of mind*, that we ever fay ' there is an impropriety in punifhing a man ' for his conduct. If the impoffibility of ' acting well has arifen from a *bad difpofi-* ' *tion* or *habit*, its having been impoffible ' with that difpofition or habit to act virtu-' oufly, is never any reafon for our forbear-' ing punifhment *.' But if it be confiftent to punifh a man for neceffary evil, or reward for neceffary good, it cannot be inconfiftent to promife or threaten, or propofe other motives to obedience †.

But you are more bold than the above writer, or indeed any other objector I have met with; for you fuppofe that God can-

---

* On Neceffity, § vi.

† See further confiderations on this fubject in Fuller's Syftems compared, Letter vi.

not

not create ' the meaneſt reptile either with
' a determination to render it miſerable, or
' with a *preſcience of its miſery* *.' So then,
not the meaneſt reptile can be miſerable, òr
the Creator muſt ceaſe to be omniſcient !—
Preſumptuous man ! wilt thou preſcribe laws
to the Supreme, and tell him he is *bound* to
make thee happy ? Surely, Sir, if made
happy, ſuch creatures as we are may be
content to owe our happineſs to the grace of
our Benefactor ! at leaſt, this is the diſpoſition of Calviniſts, and in particular of,

Yours, &c.

---

* I obſerve in the *Analytical Review* for June, that
you have, on the remonſtrance of theſe Reviewers,
endeavoured to palliate this bold aſſertion, by inſert-
ing the word *eternal*; God cannot create ' the meaneſt
' reptile—with a preſcience of its *eternal* miſery ;'
which is ſaying, God is abſolutely *obliged*, by a neceſſity of nature, to make, or endeavour to make, all
his creatures *eventually* and *eternally* happy, however
depraved and miſerable they may make themſelves.
A ſuppoſition this, which at once annihilates either the
infinity of divine Wiſdom, or the freeneſs of divine
Mercy ; and is therefore little leſs obnoxious than your
original aſſertion.

* Letters p. 27.

LETTER XIX.

Of the Poſſibility of Hereditary Depravity.

SIR,

IN the next place, you endeavour to prove the doctrine of Hereditary Depravity an impoſſibility, as utterly inconſiſtent with the conſtitution of human nature, either phyſically or metaphyſically conſidered.

Admitting the literal hiſtory of the fall, which, however you appear to doubt, you confidently enquire : ' Could the indulgence ' of this one propenſity produce, by any ' phyſical law of the conſtitution, ſuch a ' ſingular change in their natures, that they ' ſhould be neceſſitated by this change to ' procreate a race of beings directly oppoſite ' in character to the original nature infuſed ' by the immediate power of the Almighty*.' —To this I reply, that when Adam propagated human nature, it muſt neceſſarily, without a miracle, have been propagated in

* Letters, p. 101.

the

the ſtate in which it then was, and not in
that in which it formerly had been *. Thus
you are compelled to admit, that Adam was
created immortal; yet having been ſubjected
to mortality by ſin, he propagated a mortal
offspring; and the contrary would have been
againſt a fundamental law of nature, that
like begets like; and, ' Who can bring a
' clean thing out of an unclean ?'

You allow indeed, ' that a prevailing caſt
' of character may be tranſmitted to the
' *immediate offspring* †;' and I think you will
not deny that this ' prevailing caſt of cha-
' racter' may ſometimes run through two or
three ſucceſſive generations—Where then is
the impoſſibility of its being tranſmitted
further ?   As to what you ſay of this hypotheſis, attributing ' infinitely greater force
' to one particular deſire, excited and grati-
' fied in a ſingle inſtance, in *oppoſition* to the
' general character, than to the influence of
' the general character itſelf ‡,' I muſt refer
you to Mr. *Belſham*, who aſſures us, ' it is
' an invariable principle, that *one* vice ſtamps

* See above, p.234, 5.   † Letters, p. 101.
‡ Ibid. p. 102.

' a cha-

' a character vicious'—and that ' the union
' of a fingle vice with a conftellation of vir-
' tues, will contaminate them all *.' But
I hardly need have gone fo far; you yourfelf have given a fufficient anfwer. The
firft offence, you admit, ' totally obliterated
' every title to the character of innocence.
' The unfortunate pair could no longer re-
' joice in the fimplicity and purity of their
' minds. The dreadful penalty was now in-
' curred. The deed once perpetrated, in-
' evitably expofed them to the threatned
' punifhment †.' And how is it poffible
that this change fhould have no effect on
their pofterity ?

It is ufelefs and impertinent to enquire
how the firft offence produced effects fo fatal
to Adam and his pofterity. There are but
few facts of which the *modus* can be fatisfactorily explained. But it is certainly as
eafy to fhew how a fallen being fhould pro-
pagate a fallen nature as a perfect one. Nor
is it neceffary to fhew how the beafts acquired
their ferocity, &c. If we cannot account
for this fact, it will not invalidate the other.

---

* See above, p. 35, &c.   † Letters, p. 104, 5.

Your

Your remark on this point, however, fufficiently filences your objection on another;
for this ' conftitution of things is certainly
' as contrary to our primary notions of the
' divine character, as the permiffion of moral
' evil in the moral world,' however that evil
may have been introduced or propagated.

' If we confider the fubject *metaphyfically*
' we fhall be prefented,' you conceive, ' with
' objections not *lefs* formidable :' but if they
are not *more* formidable, we fhall find little
occafion to be alarmed. Firft, the doctrine
is ' not very confiftent with the ideas' we
' entertain of mind *.' A materialift, you
think, might do better; he might compare
human nature to *bread* or *cheefe*, and the
corruption of it to *leaven* or *curd*; a fmall
quantity of which might corrupt the mafs†.
We are obliged to you for this *bread and
cheefe argument*, but as we are not mate-
rialifts, we cannot ufe it ; neither are we fufficiently in want of argument to employ it,
if we could. Now comes, however, your
formidable *dilemma*, fuppofing the fpiritu-
ality of the human mind, the foul, muft be

* Letters, p. 110.   † Ib. 111.

either

either created and infufed immediately by
God, or it muft be propagated with the
body, by ordinary generation.

‘ The firft hypothefis obvioufly renders
‘ the doctrine of hereditary depravity an
‘ impoffibility. For the mind of man, the
‘ offending part, could not have been in the
‘ loins of our firft parents, when they com-
‘ mitted the offence, and therefore could
‘ not have been contaminated by it. The
‘ fpirit of every individual proceeding imme-
‘ diately from the hands of his Maker, muft
‘ be as pure, as refined, and as free from fin,
‘ as the foul of Adam on the day of his
‘ creation . . . According to this hypothefis,
‘ therefore, the genuine doctrine of original
‘ fin muft be renounced. For, whatever
‘ pollution the foul may contract when com-
‘ pelled to inhabit the corporeal frame, this
‘ muft fimply be a fin of infection, not he-
‘ reditary guilt . . . And fuppofing this to be
‘ fo infufferably vile as to pollute and deprave
‘ every foul that enters, that foul cannot be
‘ charged with hereditary guilt, however it
‘ may be pitied for being conftrained to oc-
‘ cupy fo improper a dwelling *.’

* Letters, p. 112---14.

The

The latter part of this reafoning is foreign and irrelevant to the fubject, becaufe we do not place the depravity of human nature in the material fyftem, nor do we refolve it into a mere infection or pollution; and the former part goes upon the fuppofition of human depravity being an evil pofitively implanted, whereas the whole is completely to be accounted for upon another principle, which I fhall explain in the accurate terms of the judicious Pref. *Edwards*.

' The cafe with man (he fays) was plain-
' ly this: when God made man at firft, he
' implanted in him two kinds of principles.
' There was an inferior kind, which may be
' called natural, being the principles of mere
' human nature; fuch as felf-love, with
' thofe natural appetites and paffions which
' belong to the nature of man: .... Thefe,
' when alone, and left to themfelves, are
' what the fcriptures fometimes call *flefh* *.
' Befide thefe there were fuperior principles,
' fpiritual, holy, and divine, ... which are
' called the *divine nature* †. Thefe principles
' may, in fome fenfe, be called fupernatural,

---

* Rom. viii. 6.   † 2 Pet. i. 4.

being

' being (however concreated or connate, yet)
' such as are above those principles that are
' essentially . . . . connected with *mere human*
' *nature*, and such as depend on man's union
' and communion with God. . . . . When
' man sinned, and broke God's covenant,
' and fell under his curse, these superior
' principles left his heart : for indeed God
' then left him : . . . . the Holy Spirit, that
' divine inhabitant, forsook the house . . . .
' Therefore immediately the superior divine
' principle wholly ceased ; so light ceases in
' a room when the candle is withdrawn :
' and thus man was left in a state of dark-
' ness, woeful corruption, and ruin ; nothing
' but flesh without Spirit : [i. e. the fleshly
' principle without the Holy Spirit] and as
' Adam's nature became corrupt without
' God's implanting or infusing any evil thing
' into his nature ; so does the nature of
' his posterity. God dealing with Adam as
' the head of his posterity, and treating them
' as one, he deals with his posterity as having
' *all sinned in him.* And, therefore, as God
' withdrew spiritual communion and his vital
' gracious influence from the common head,
' so he withholds the same from all the
' members,

'members, as they come into exiftence:
' whereby they come into the world mere
' *flefh* [in the fenfe above explained] and
' entirely under the government of natural
' and inferior principles; and fo become
' corrupt, as Adam did *.'

Now if the depravity of human nature
arife from a defect only of that in human
nature, which was loft and forfeited by the
fin of our firft parent, how is it an abfolute
impoffibility?

As to the other hypothefis of the propagation, or traduction of fouls, this you feem
to think might account for it; but then it
is itfelf attended with its *difficulties,* which
is alfo true of every theological fyftem or
opinion. You will readily admit this to be
the cafe in every point connected with the
doctrine of fpirits, and I think you muft
admit that the idea of *confcious matter* is attended with its difficulties, and thofe of no
fmall confideration. Muft we therefore deny
that it is poffible to *think,* becaufe both the
doctrines of fpirits, and of materialifm, are
attended with their difficulties? Yet furely

* Edwards on Orig. Sin. Part iv. chap. 2.

this

this would be as rational as to pretend that human nature cannot be depraved, becaufe we know not how that depravity is communicated through the fpecies.

As to the confequences faftened upon this fyftem, that it fuppofes ' Myriads and my-' riads of miferable embrios, that never faw ' the light of the fun will as infallibly be ' plunged into the flames of hell, as the ' moft abandoned of our fpecies ; and [that] ' every germ that poffeffes a phyfical poffi-' bility of exifting in this world fhall, with-' out doubt, perifh everlaftingly in the ' next ! ! ! *' This confequence, I fay, is purely and entirely your own ; and the three notes of attention you have added only call our admiration to your talent of disfiguring the fyftem of an opponent, fince certainly no Calvinift will admit your inference, nor does it belong to our hypothefis. For,

1. To maintain that the human race *merit* the divine difpleafure in a future ftate, and that they actually *fuffer* it, are very different pofitions. That infants may be expofed to God's righteous judgments, is indeed gene-

* Letters, p. 115.

rally

rally maintained by Calvinifts, and is ftrongly fupported by the fact of their fuffering
the agonies of difeafe and death : but I know
of very few divines in the prefent age, who
maintain or fuppofe that a fingle child of
Adam ever fuffered, or will fuffer, the punifhments of a future ftate, without having
confirmed and aggravated his original guilt
by actual tranfgreffion.

2. Your zeal to blacken Calvinifm carries
you into an extreme of abfurdity, of which
you do not feem to be aware. For how can
unconfcious embryos and unanimated germs
of exiftence be plunged into the flames of
hell? or if that were poffible, what would
be the utmoft amount of the fufferings of
myriads of unconfcious, unanimated germs
of poffible exiftence?—Is not this multi-
plying words without ideas, and attempting
to terrify us with a rhetorical flourifh upon
nothing?—Once more, I remain,

Yours, &c.

LETTER XX.

Recapitulation of Evidence—Conclusion.

Sir;

HAVING gone through what I judged moſt important, both in your Letters and Mr. Belſham's, it may not be improper to conclude with drawing into one view the principal proofs and arguments for the truth of *Original,* or as you term it, ' Hereditary ' Depravity,' as they lay ſcattered in ſeveral of my Letters, and ſubjoin ſuch obſervations as may occur in the recapitulation.

The main queſtion ſeems to divide itſelf into two branches—the *extent* of human depravity, and the *cauſe* of it.

On the firſt queſtion, we have ſeen the uniform repreſentation of the ſcriptures of both Teſtaments, from Moſes to Paul, to be, that human nature is univerſally and totally depraved. The heart is deceitful above all things, and deſperately wicked—the fountain of all iniquity. The thoughts are evil—only and continually evil—even from our youth

I i   up.

up. And to this perfectly corresponds the conduct of mankind. They are all gone astray—every one turned to his own way. There is none righteous, none that doeth good, no not one *. And when the world at large is described, either by our Lord or his apostles, it is in such terms as the following. *Jesus* says, ' The world cannot hate ' you, but me it hateth, because I testify of ' it, that its deeds are evil.' *John* declares, ' The whole world lieth in wickedness †.'

* See above, p. 19—22.—Two things are objected to this statement: 1. It is like describing nature by its storms and tempests. [Letters, p. 79.] Be it so : if storms and tempests occur in any certain latitude every day, and throughout all the seasons, must we not conclude them natural to the climate?—2. Mankind are mixed characters, good as well as evil. [Letters, p. 94.] True; but scripture ascribes the bad to nature, and the good to grace. As to the case of children, [Letters, p. 91.] they are described as good only by comparison, or in a certain respect. ' Folly ' (or sin) is bound up in the heart of a child,' but it is gradually unfolded. Children are patterns of humility and docility, and with this view were recommended to the disciples. ' Of such is the kingdom of heaven,' means, probably, that the subjects of Christ's kingdom must be regenerated, or born again, and thus become little children.

† John vii. 7.—1 John v. 19.

2. The

The other point to be confidered is the *caufe* of this depravity, whether it be the one, uniform, and fimple caufe affigned in fcripture, or whether each individual is feparately and diftinctly contaminated and depraved. That it is the former, I conclude from the following confiderations, moft of which are recapitulatory.

(1.) Previous to the fall, I obferve, that human nature is defcribed in terms very different, and even oppofite to what are employed afterwards. Then every thing created was pronounced very good; and man, in particular, to be created in the image of God, which is elfewhere faid to confift, principally, in knowledge and in righteoufnefs*.

(2.) Sin and death are exprefsly faid to have been introduced by our firft parents : for ' by one man fin entered into the world, ' and death by fin : and fo death paffed upon ' all men, for that [or *in whom*] 'all have ' finned †.

3. Adam is frequently fpoken of in fcripture, not as a private ifolated individual, but as a public perfon, the federal head of his

* Above, p. 49.   † P. 222.

pofterity.

pofterity. In this view he is compared to Chrift, the fecond Adam, by whom life and immortality are communicated to mankind, as death and mifery by the former *.

4. It is evident, notwithftanding your objections, that Adam's pofterity do partake the confequences of his fin in labour, dif-eafe, and death, and that thefe conftituted, at leaft, part of his punifhment ; and if involved in part of his punifhment, why not in the whole ? Indeed, it feems neceffary to admit that we are fome way implicated in his crime, from our being involved in his punifhment, otherwife we muft fuppofe that the Lord punifhes the innocent with the guilty †:—and ' that be far from thee, O ' Lord!'—This argument is particularly for-cible as it refpects the cafe of Children ‡.

5. The mifery and death fuffered by the pofterity of Adam, are reprefented in fcrip-ture as the proper ' wages,' or defert of fin. Whatever therefore may be this demerit, it feems entailed upon us as the proper reward of his tranfgreffion §.

---

* Above, p. 229.　† P. 277.　‡ P .222.
§ P. 229.

6. We

6. We are reprefented as born in fin—children of wrath by nature—tranfgreffors from the womb—depraved and defiled from the birth *.

7. In confequence of this depravity, human nature is reprefented as prone to fin, and with a propenfity to moral evil; fo much fo, as without converting grace to be incapable of receiving, underftanding, or loving the things of God †.

8. Good men, under both difpenfations, confeffed and bewailed the remains of this corruption, which they defcribe as the fource of a continual warfare within them, the flefh lufting againft the fpirit, and the fpirit againft the flefh ‡.

9. The defperate condition of human nature by the fall, might be farther argued from the extraordinary provifion made for its recovery in the incarnation, fufferings, and death of the Son of God: but as thefe articles are contefted and denied by you, as well as the depravity I would infer from them, I cannot here juftly avail myfelf of this topic.

---

*P. 21, 231, &c.   † P. 169.   ‡ P. 29, 33, &c.

The

The principal objections urged by you, and by Mr. Belsham, have been also more or less considered and obviated. There is indeed, a certain class of objections to which I have judged it necessary to give the less attention, as they lie equally strong against the Necessarian as the Calvinistic System ; and therefore cannot with propriety be urged by Unitarian Writers, who generally, if I mistake not, adopt that hypothesis. Those here referred to, are such as—the difficulty of shewing the equity of God in requiring purity unattainable in our depraved state— in punishing sin necessarily committed—or in inviting sinners to mercy which they cannot accept without his grace. These difficulties seem to arise from our present contracted powers and information ; and are perhaps insurmountable without a new revelation, and enlarged capacities.

But it appears to me highly indecorous for creatures to contend with their Creator, and more so for sinners to dispute with their almighty Judge, or their compassionate Saviour. Let me, therefore, intreat you, Sir, and gentlemen of your sentiments, to speculate with more reverence and caution on

these

thefe myfterious fubjects. It is of little confequence in what terms you treat the obfervations or remonftrances of a fellow mortal.
The potfherd may ftrive with the potfherds
of the earth ; but woe unto him ' that ftriv-
' eth with his Maker * !'

As to myfelf, Sir, though I am not inti-
midated by the idea of meeting you in the
field of controverfy, with the lawful wea-
pons of fcripture and fober reafon, yet, to
accompany you as a fellow fupplicant at the
throne of grace, would give far greater pleafure and fatisfaction to

Your fincere and humble fervant

for the Truth's fake,

T. W.

* Ifa. xlv. 9:

August, 1, 1799.

Early in December next, will be published,

IN ONE NEAT VOLUME, OCTAVO,

PRICE TO SUBSCRIBERS, 4s. IN BOARDS; TO OTHERS, 5s.

(With an Elegant FRONTISPIECE, *illustrative of the Imagery of the Poem.)*

THE
SONG OF SONGS,

WHICH IS

SOLOMON's;

A NEW TRANSLATION,

ATTEMPTED IN THE MANNER OF BP. LOWTH's ISAIAH,

WITH SELECT CRITICAL NOTES,

AND

AN EVANGELICAL COMMENTARY;

ON A PLAN ENTIRELY NEW.

TO WHICH ARE PREFIXED,

INTRODUCTORY ESSAYS:

I. On the Origin of LANGUAGE, of POETRY, and of ALLEGORY.
II. On the Nature, Design, and Divine Authority of SOLOMON's SONG.

By T. WILLIAMS.

*** Subscribers' Names will continue to be received where this Work
is sold, until the end of September.

Written by the same Author, and sold by the same Booksellers.

I. AN HISTORIC DEFENCE OF EXPERIMENTAL RELIGION:
in which the Doctrine of Divine Influences is particularly considered,
and supported by the Authority of Scripture, and the Experience of the
wisest and best Men in all Ages and Countries. 2 vols. 12mo. price 6s.
boards.   N. B. This Work is enriched with Anecdotes and Biographi-
cal Sketches of more than 250 eminent Persons.

II. THE AGE OF INFIDELITY, in Two Parts, answering the Two
Parts of *Paine's* ' Age of Reason.' Part I. Price 1s. 6d.—Part II. 2s. 6d.
III. THE AGE OF CREDULITY, in answer to Mr. Halhed's Defence
of Brothers. Price 1s.

IV. REASONS FOR FAITH IN REVEALED RELIGION; opposed
to Mr. *Hollis's* ' Reasons for Scepticism.' Price 1s.

V. INFANT SALVATION: an Essay to prove the Salvation of all
who die in Infancy. Price 6d.

VI. THE MISSIONARY, a Poem, in Blank Verse: with Hints on
the Propagation of the Gospel. Price 6d. 12mo.